P9-DNL-623

The Girls of Firefly Cabin

Cynthia Ellingsen

Albert Whitman & Company
Chicago, Illinois

PH CASS COUNTY PUBLIC LIBRARY
400 E. MECHANIC
HARRISONVILLE, MO 64701

0 0022 0583400 1

Library of Congress Cataloging-in-Publication
data is on file with the publisher.

Text copyright © 2019 by Cynthia Ellingsen
First published in the United States of America
in 2019 by Albert Whitman & Company
ISBN 978-0-8075-2939-3
All rights reserved. No part of this book may be reproduced or transmitted in
any form or by any means, electronic or mechanical, including photocopying,
recording, or by any information storage and retrieval system,
without permission in writing from the publisher.

Printed in the United States of America.
10 9 8 7 6 5 4 3 2 1 LB 24 23 22 21 20 19

Cover images copyright © by Yodchai Prominn/Shutterstock, jldeines/iStock

For more information about Albert Whitman & Company,
visit our web site at www.albertwhitman.com.

100 years of Albert Whitman & Company
Celebrate with us in 2019!

To Hazel, who fills my heart
with joy, love, and laughter

Chapter One

Lauren clutched the brochure for the Blueberry Pine Camp for Girls close to her heart. The airplane landed with a whirring roar and taxied down the runway. She let out a breath and looked down at the cover of the camp advertisement.

Four girls stood in a row. They wore matching grins and the traditional camp uniform: green knee socks, navy buttondown shirts, and green corduroy trousers that ended below the knee. The campers posed beneath lush pine trees, their eyes bright with friendship and shared secrets.

It was the perfect picture. Probably from the perfect summer, the type Lauren imagined other girls—rich girls with families—got to have. Lauren, on the other hand, typically spent her summers doing kitchen duty and changing diapers at Shady Acres, the group foster home where she lived.

When she'd won an essay contest to attend the Blueberry Pine Camp for Girls, she had felt like the luckiest girl alive. Going to camp was a dream come true. It was finally happening, and she couldn't wait to start the best summer of her life.

"Traverse City, Michigan," announced the flight attendant, and some of the passengers applauded.

Lauren wiped the sweat off her hands and tucked the brochure into the front pocket of her backpack. She couldn't contain the smile on her face as the flight attendant walked her through the airport to retrieve her luggage. Her thrift shop suitcase with the rip in the green fabric sat on the luggage carousel, waiting for her like a good friend.

Nearby, a man in a plaid golf cap held a sign that read WELCOME, LAUREN WILLIAMS! Lauren chewed her nails while the adults swapped paperwork.

"Have a wonderful time at camp, Lauren." The flight attendant handed her a water and a few packets of pretzels.

"Ready, kid?" The driver gave her a big smile. He put her frayed suitcase in the trunk of a black town car and held open the door, like she was somebody special.

Tall pine trees flashed by the windows as he pulled onto the road. Fluffy clouds dotted the bright blue sky like something out of a picture book. The vibrant colors were so different from the pastel landscape back in Arizona.

The driver glanced in the rearview mirror. "You go to camp every year?"

"No, sir." Lauren squeezed her hands. "This is my first time. I...I won an essay contest."

Winning was such a shock. It had taken five weeks of writing and rewriting an essay explaining why she wanted to be a part of Blueberry Pine. She had been embarrassed in the end, convinced the judges would laugh and throw it away.

Three weeks later, she'd received a surprise letter in the mail. She'd read and reread it until the paper was smooth and worn.

It said:

Dear Lauren,

Congratulations! "Searching for Sisterhood" was selected as the winning entry for the Beatrice Hunt Scholarship Award to the Blueberry Pine Camp for Girls. Please accept this letter as an invitation for your eight-week stay in Firefly Cabin. Once your acceptance is confirmed, we'll send a stipend for travel and clothing. Thank you for your heartfelt words, and congratulations again!

With a bright Blueberry Pine welcome,
Carol Kennedy
Director of Outreach Services

"That's wonderful, kid," the driver said. "What a great opportunity."

"It is." Lauren gave a serious nod. "I live in a group foster home, so I was lucky to get permission to go."

He raised an eyebrow. "You an orphan?"

Lauren hated how people reacted when they found out

she didn't have a family. It would be nice, for once, if no one knew.

In fact...

Lauren sat up straight. The girls at camp wouldn't know unless she decided to tell them.

"Hey, do you drive a lot of the campers?" she asked.

He shrugged. "Only the special ones."

"Then can you do me a favor?" She leaned over the front seat. "I...I really don't want any of the girls to know I live in a group home. I'd like to pretend to be someone else for a while."

The driver's eyes met hers in the rearview mirror. "Sure, kid. Your secret is safe with me."

He clicked the radio to an oldies station and hummed along. She pulled out the creased camp brochure and flipped through it like a favorite book. Finally, the car crested a hill, and a brilliant blue lake appeared below. The road leading down to it was lined with trees and—oh gosh!—the colorful flags pictured in the brochure:

A Bright Blueberry Pine Welcome

Sunshine: One Mile

Blueberry Pine Camp for Girls: Join the Fun

The car pulled into a long dirt driveway. A sign made of crisscrossed logs hung over the entrance. In wood-burnt letters, it read Est. 1948.

Lauren rolled down the window, and her red hair whipped in the wind. The drive down the dirt road smelled like pine needles, wet dirt, and something sweet—maybe fresh-cut grass or wildflowers. Her stomach jumped with excitement as the car approached a small, wooden building, where two older girls stood with clipboards.

The blond girl turned to greet a car on the opposite side, while a tall Asian girl greeted Lauren. She wore her long black hair in a sleek ponytail and had a mouth full of braces. In spite of the braces, she blew purple bubbles with a large piece of chewing gum.

"A bright Blueberry Pine welcome! I'm Cassandra." She shook Lauren's hand through the open window of the car. "What cabin are you in?"

"Firefly Cabin." Lauren beamed. "I'm a Firefly."

According to the camp website, which Lauren had studied with great care, Blueberry Pine campers ranged in age from ten to thirteen. There were two cabin clusters for each age bracket, with the exception of the ten-year-olds, who only had one, due to lower enrollment. The ten-year-olds lived in cabins named after fruit; the eleven-year-olds were insects; the twelve-year-olds were trees; and the oldest girls, birds.

"I've been excited to be a Firefly for weeks," Lauren admitted.

"That's great news, because I'm a Firefly, too," Cassandra said. "I'm your counselor."

Lauren's eyes widened. "It's so nice to meet you!" She

couldn't believe she was talking to her cabin counselor. It felt like meeting a celebrity.

Cassandra pointed at the blond girl. "We all have different duties throughout the day. I'm on check-in duty now, but I'll be back to the cabin before the welcome ceremony and bonfire this afternoon." She studied a page of photographs on her clipboard. "You must be...Lauren."

Cassandra gave her a fist bump. "Let me get you your welcome packet with all the information you need, including a map to the cabin." She stepped into the tiny building and returned with a folder packed with papers. "You're the first of the Fireflies to arrive, so make yourself at home. There are all sorts of activities planned throughout the day, like soccer games and a water balloon toss on the main lawn, so have fun and I'll see you soon."

Lauren's driver gave a friendly wave to the counselors and headed back up the hill to the main camp.

"This is incredible," Lauren breathed, leaning over the front seat.

It was as if the camp website had sprung to life. The main area had a bright green lawn dotted with picnic tables and benches, next to a small building with a sign that read CANTEEN. From her online research, Lauren knew it was a snack bar. Campers were already lined up for ice-cream cones, talking and laughing with friends. Nearby, wood-chip-covered pathways led toward clusters of log cabins. The lake—oh, it was so blue!—gleamed at the edge of it all, with pine trees reflected in its glass-like surface.

The driver pulled over and got out of the car to retrieve Lauren's suitcase from the trunk. Finally standing on camp ground, Lauren opened her worn change purse and held out the ten-dollar bill her housemother had given her for gratuities. The driver waved it away.

"Keep it, kid." He climbed back into the car. "Buy yourself a treat."

Lauren's mouth dropped open. "No, I…I have to give you a tip."

The driver leaned out the window. "How about this for a tip: the world don't owe you any favors. So, when it does you one, smile and say 'thank you.'" He touched the brim of his cap. "Have fun at camp."

Lauren couldn't believe her luck. Ten whole dollars?!

I can buy ice cream!

Heck, with ten dollars she could buy ice cream for herself *and* her new friends. She waved at the driver, grinning from ear to ear, until he was out of sight.

Turning, she looked out across Blueberry Pine. It was just perfect. Birds chirped, bugs droned with the steady song of summer, and she blinked back ridiculous tears.

The driver is right. The world doesn't owe me any favors. Sometimes, though, it comes through.

With a smile, she whispered, "Thank you."

Without a doubt, summer at the Blueberry Pine Camp for Girls was going to be the most exciting adventure of her life.

Chapter Two

Isla hid in a corner of the general store, careful not to touch a thing. Her parents had insisted on stopping for handcrafted ice cream on the way to camp, which sounded good at the time. That is, until they'd picked this dump, where Isla spotted a sign that read LIVE BAIT…and noticed buckets of scaly black worms in the fridge.

Bleh.

Just like the idea of going to camp.

Isla wanted to spend summer like she always did: visiting the Met, running her Internet business, and working through the top one hundred American Library Classics. But this year her parents had planned a trip to Europe. Instead of allowing her to spend the summer with her grandparents like her older brothers (lucky brothers with their summer rugby team), her parents had decided to ship her off to camp, claiming it would be good for her college applications.

The Ivy Leagues were six years away. Isla wanted a quality education, but please. Camp sounded as disgusting as this store.

Mosquitoes? Bunk beds? *Latrines?*

Uggh.

Plus, the past few weeks had been a torment of secret worries: What would the girls in her cabin be like? What if her inhaler didn't work? Would she be okay with her parents approximately 4,150 miles away?

The situation was stressful beyond words.

"Isla!" Her mother's voice trilled through the store. Too loud, like always. Her parents were hotshot corporate lawyers in Manhattan and (mistakenly) thought everyone wanted to hear what they had to say.

Isla ducked her head and rushed down the aisle. Turning a corner, she smacked into someone. "Sorry." She put out a hand to steady herself. "I…"

The words died on her lips. Her hand rested on the chest of the most beautiful boy she'd ever seen. He had dark, curly hair and laughing brown eyes, and he smelled like grape Jolly Ranchers.

Isla dropped her hand, too stunned to speak.

The boy grinned. "Nice outfit."

He, too, wore a camp uniform, which meant he was attending the boys' camp across the lake. Her heart started to pound.

"I'm Jordan." When she didn't respond, he added, "You know, we could be twins, dressed like this. Maybe we could share clothes."

Just then, her mother swept around the corner and thrust a chocolate shake into her hands. "Try this," she proclaimed. "It's extraordinary."

Quickly, Isla turned away from Jordan. She wasn't allowed to even think about boys until she was fifteen, which meant four more years to go. Her mother would ground her for life if she knew the thoughts running through her head. Things like I wonder if I'll see him at camp? or What would it be like to kiss him?

The idea sent her into such a panic that she didn't get a good grip on the cup. The lid popped off, and chocolate doused the front of her shirt. The boy burst out laughing.

Mortified, Isla chose the only logical option: she darted for the door, down the wooden steps, and straight to her parents' car. Her mother hurried behind her.

"Young lady, stop right there!" The locks on the Cadillac beeped shut. "You are *not* getting in my rental car like that."

Isla stood shivering as her mother extracted a starched button-down shirt from the Louis Vuitton luggage in the trunk.

"They'll have a bathroom in the store." Her mother handed it to her. "Go change."

In the bathroom? In that gross store?

"Mommy, no," Isla pleaded. "Let me just—"

"Now."

How embarrassing. Of course the cute boy chose that very moment to open the screened door.

And her mother chose that very moment to shout, "YOU'LL NEED ANOTHER BRA!" Like something out of a nightmare, she pulled a lacy white training bra out of Isla's luggage and waved it like a flag.

The boy's hand froze on the doorframe.

Isla's mother sailed over and shoved it into her hands. "That young man is holding the door," she scolded. "Don't make him stand there all day."

Isla scuttled up the steps, heart pounding. She couldn't help but glance his way. His dark eyes locked onto hers.

"I take back what I said about trading clothes," he murmured.

Her cheeks flushed bright red. She ducked past him, wishing she didn't have to change. There was a real chance that the moment she took off the icy shirt, her body would burst into flames.

Chapter Three

Archer sat cross-legged on a bed of grass and pine needles in the center of camp and picked at the black polish on her thumbnail. A steady pulse of insects chirped in the background, and the air smelled like moldy bread.

Plucking a piece of sweet clover from the ground, Archer stuck it into her mouth and looked up at her sister. Makayla was perched on the edge of a bench. Her blue eyes shined with tears as she acted like it might just kill her to say goodbye to their parents.

Please.

Makayla wouldn't even call their parents until she needed money for snacks.

There was a burst of laughter from a nearby table, and Archer looked over. Four girls sat together sharing three different flavors of ice cream.

Oh, wow. For a moment, camp seemed promising. It would be fun to have friends like that. Then reality set in.

Everyone will hate you, like always. Thanks to her.

Makayla was on her fourth and final year of camp. That meant she knew everyone and most likely had a tribe of minions eager to do her bidding. Humiliating Archer would be at the top of their list. Really, it wouldn't be that hard, because Archer was completely new to all of this.

Band practice had kept Archer safe from camp last year. But she had quit the band without weighing the consequences. Now, here she was, about to be a sitting duck for her sister.

Archer's mother got to her feet. "Honey, can we get a hug?"

The invitation made her practically fall into her mother's arms. It wasn't like she was a wimp or anything, but she wanted to go home. The idea of being with strangers for eight whole weeks—and at the mercy of her sister—was terrifying.

"Hang in there, okay?" Her mother brushed her fingers over the blue and purple streaks in Archer's hair. "Eight weeks isn't forever."

"Tell that to someone being eaten slowly by a boa constrictor," Archer said.

It was something she wouldn't mind seeing happen to her sister.

Her father chuckled. "Have fun, kiddo." He gave an awkward punch to her arm, and her parents headed for the parking lot.

Immediately, Makayla iced her with a look.

"Okay, loser. Here are the rules," she snapped. "Do *not* speak to me unless I speak to you, and do not tell a *soul* we are related. Got it?"

The rules were the same at school. By now, Archer was used to it, but she'd half hoped camp would be different. Clearly that wasn't the case.

"I'd rather eat bugs than tell people we're sisters," Archer shot back. "Because people would assume I'm as fake as you."

"Mmm." Makayla's catlike eyes appraised her. "Your hair looks hideous. Do yourself a favor and set it on fire." She waggled her fingers. "Have a great summer."

Rage welled up inside of Archer. Before she could fire off an appropriate comeback, a gaggle of pretty girls raced onto the green lawn. The cool kids, no doubt. They tackled Makayla in a group hug, screaming with delight.

"Bluebirds!" Makayla cried, which was the name of her stupid cabin.

The girls jumped up and down. "We're finally Bluebirds!" they squealed, flapping their arms as if they were wings. The display should have been embarrassing, but they made it look like the most fun thing ever.

"Uh, hello." Suddenly, a blond with mirrored aviators noticed Archer. "Are you friends with Makayla?"

Makayla scoffed. "Blue Hair started following me around the moment I got here."

Great. Now everyone would think she was a total freak.

Archer rushed toward one of the wooden pathways, but not before her sister got in one more jab.

"She looks like a My Little Pony," Makayla trilled. "The zombie version."

The Bluebirds chirped with laughter, and shame crushed Archer's heart.

Safe in the cool darkness of the forest, she stopped and looked up at the trees.

Am I really that awful? Why does my own sister hate me so much?

Their relationship hadn't always been bad. For most of their lives, they were happy to ride bikes and play Barbies and video games together. Everything changed when they moved to the suburbs of Chicago, and Makayla started junior high.

It was like, overnight, Makayla didn't want to build forts in the backyard or dance silly in the kitchen. She made friends with the type of mean girls they'd never liked back in their old school, started wearing makeup, and begged their parents for a smartphone. From then on, she spent every second on group texts.

Things got even worse when Archer joined her at the junior high. The first day of school, her sister had spread a rumor that Archer had a weird skin condition, contagious within three feet. Everyone had stayed far away.

Why would camp be any different?

If only she could hide under the weeping willow tree by the lake for the rest of the summer. Unfortunately, there were probably too many snakes, so she decided to find her cabin and see how bad this would be.

When the path opened next to the lake, Archer stopped. The water mirrored the color of the sky, and it was surrounded by fir trees. Silent and still, the scene filled her with a sense of longing to sketch it on her arm with a Sharpie.

A burst of laughter snapped her out of her reverie. Quickly, she moved aside for a group of girls barreling down the trail. They weren't looking at a map, so they were probably second- or third-year campers. They barely noticed her as they pushed by.

With a sigh, Archer looked down at the map. The path leading to Firefly Cabin was marked with a wood-burnt drawing of a sun. She followed it to a cluster of five log cabins, each marked by a colorful flag bearing an image of its namesake: Firefly, Dragonfly, Butterfly, Ladybug, and Cicada.

Archer found the Firefly flag and climbed the steps of the cabin, her stomach clenched with nerves. She peeked through the dusty screen door. Inside, a group of girls chatted like old friends. She had two thoughts: one, they all knew one another, and two, they were probably as snotty as the Bluebirds.

Sure enough, the first girl she made eye contact with could have been Makayla's twin. The girl was Disney Channel gorgeous, with stick-straight silver-blond hair, flushed cheeks, and bright blue eyes. She didn't say hi, just went back to tacking up a lavender sheet around her bunk bed like a curtain.

Don't worry. I don't want to be your friend, either.

The cabin was twice the size of her room back home, but cleaner. It had two sets of bunk beds, a cot for their counselor, a community area, and a bathroom sink. The shelves next to the sink already held toothbrushes. Based on the yellow case next to a tube of toothpaste, Archer wasn't the only one who wore a retainer.

That sense of relief vanished the moment she noticed the bathroom, a small closet by the sink. There was a three-inch gap between the floor and the door! How could she use the bathroom if everyone could hear what she was doing?

Archer was about to make a home under that weeping willow after all when a whirlwind of enthusiasm rushed forward.

"Hi, I'm Lauren!" The girl thrust out her hand, her gray eyes wide set and friendly.

"Hey." Archer gave an awkward wave. "Archer."

"Cool name!" Lauren bounced up and down. "It's so super-great to meet you."

Super-great?

This girl was as eager as a golden retriever. Clearly this was a setup for some joke.

Archer crossed her arms. "If you say so."

To her surprise, Lauren pulled her into the room.

"Come meet everyone!" She pointed at a pale girl with dark hair and straight-cut bangs. "That's Isla."

Isla gave a stiff wave, like a princess in a parade or something.

"And..." Lauren beamed at the blond girl. "That's Jade."

Jade spritzed her bed with a rose-scented perfume.

"Yuck." Archer waved at the air. "That smells like my grandmother's underwear."

Everyone laughed. Well, everyone except Jade. But thanks

to the laughter, the cabin felt more comfortable, like it belonged to Archer now too.

Lauren pointed to the bunk right above Jade's. "Too bad that's your bed."

Sure enough, Archer's suitcase rested next to a thin wool blanket; old pillow; and starched, white bedsheets. Its colorful stickers shouted "Mean People Suck" and "Artificial Intelligence BFF," which suddenly seemed too aggressive in the small space.

"Well, now that we're all here..." Lauren did a silly little dance. "I have a surprise for the Fireflies!" She rushed to the bunk on the opposite side of the room and snapped open an old-fashioned suitcase. She waved everyone over to a small table. It was painted bright red, with blue- and green-painted chairs.

"I'd like to call to order the first official meeting of the Fireflies."

Archer brushed a few dead beetles off the table and onto the floor. The pale girl (Isla?) cringed but tentatively took a seat. Jade continued arranging her drawer beneath the bed.

"You can listen from over there, Jade," Lauren called, cheerful as the sun. "So, I have dreamed about this moment, about meeting each one of you, from the very second I became a part of this cabin. I think the four of us are going to be the best of friends. Sisters. And since we're the girls of Firefly Cabin"— Lauren opened her hands to reveal a bunch of string—"I made us friendship bracelets."

Chapter Four

Friendship bracelets? Jade cringed. *How am I going to get out of this one?*

Her cabinmates were crowded together like best friends, oohing and ahhing. Even from across the room, Jade could tell the bracelets were works of art.

Friendship bracelets were the one thing she wouldn't—couldn't—wear, and this sweet, eager redhead had to make it a thing. How could she get out of this without looking like a jerk? It would be impossible, so her best bet was to try to breeze past the situation as quickly as possible.

Jade knelt down on the scratchy wooden floor and unpacked her last piece of clothing. It startled her to see her scrapbook at the bottom of the suitcase, and she brushed her hand over the worn cover. It was hard to believe she and Kiara had started the book when they were only six years old.

A shadow fell over her shoulder, and Jade jumped.

"Here you go," Lauren sang, handing her a bracelet.

Sure enough, it was pretty incredible. The bracelet was

hand-braided from heavy string in navy, light blue, and white. In the center sparkled a firefly, embroidered in silver thread.

It must have taken Lauren some serious time to make these. Jade wanted to compliment her, but the words sat like a lump in her throat. The moment Lauren turned back to the other girls, Jade slid the bracelet into the drawer.

Immediately, the girl with the chip on her shoulder stalked across the room and glared at her. "Why aren't you putting on your bracelet?"

Jade stood up. "I don't want to ruin it."

"You can't ruin it." Lauren rushed back over. "Friendship bracelets are pretty dur—" She stopped, her eyes falling on the collection of friendship bracelets tied to Jade's wrist. "Oh. I guess you know that."

Jade almost caved. Until she remembered Kiara tying each bracelet to her wrist, saying, "Best friends forever."

"Lauren, I'm sorry." She rubbed the goose bumps on her arms. "I already have a best friend. We wear bracelets only from each other. It's cool, though. Thank you."

Hurt colored Lauren's freckled face. "Yours are nicer. I understand."

Jade frowned. Yes, some of her bracelets were store-bought with leather accents and silver charms, but that didn't have anything to do with it.

"I like yours," Jade insisted. "For real."

Lauren raised her eyebrows. "Okay." She sat with Isla, looking dejected.

If I could only call Kiara and ask for an exception.

Of course, that was ridiculous.

Trees creaked outside the window, and an army of bugs banged against the screen. A burst of laughter echoed from one of the cabins next door and Lauren glanced over, as though envious of the sound.

Archer cleared her throat. "Well, speaking of presents..." She grabbed her suitcase off the top bunk and produced a gigantic jar of Swedish Fish, followed by a grocery bag jam-packed with junk food. "This is for all of us."

Except you, her haughty look seemed to say to Jade.

The bag was stuffed with Power Bars in shiny gold wrappers, skinny cans of Pringles, packs of gum, M&M's, Milk Duds, Sour Patch Kids...Archer plopped the whole thing on the table to share.

"You guys, snacks are not allowed." Isla wrung her hands. "The handouts said they attract rodents."

"Please." Archer scoffed. "My sis—I mean, a girl I know had her mother send care packages every week. It's fine. I bet there's not a mouse within five hundred miles of this place."

Lauren gave a vigorous nod. "Camp is too perfect for mice."

"Okay, but it could attract bears," Isla pressed.

Archer grinned. "Then we'd better hurry up and eat it."

With that, Archer and Lauren tore into the snacks like they hadn't seen food in weeks. Isla watched with dismay, quick to wipe up any crumbs that landed on the table.

Well, good. At least they each have something else to focus on other than me.

Jade climbed into her bed, tucking a corner of her lavender sheet into the edge of the bottom bunk. The effect was a dark, cave-like shelter. She had just collapsed against the thin pillow for a nap, when someone hissed, "Is she being *serious* right now?"

Boots stomped across the wooden floor. Sunlight flooded the bed, and the girl with blue and purple hair stood over her, nostrils flaring.

"You don't want to be a part of this cabin, do you?" she demanded.

I don't want to be a part of anything.

Her life was over; it had been for months. But this horrible girl didn't deserve an explanation.

"You do you," Jade told her. "I just want to be left alone." She pulled the sheet back around her bed. To her absolute shock, the girl yanked it down and threw it onto the floor.

Jade gripped the edge of her pillow. For the first time in months, she felt something stronger than grief. Fear, maybe? Or was it rage?

"It's obvious you don't want to be a Firefly," the girl shouted, "so get your things, take your stinky attitude, and get out!"

Lauren leaped to her feet. "Hold on. Jade didn't say she doesn't want to be a part of Firefly Cabin."

"Look at her," the girl scoffed, the smell of sour cream and onion Pringles strong on her breath. "She doesn't have to say it."

"You know what?" Jade twisted the pillow case tightly around her hand. "I *don't* want to be a Firefly. Not if you're one too."

Lauren's freckled face was beet-red, as if she were fighting too. "You guys," she wailed. "We're supposed to be best friends. Sisters! What are you doing?"

The room fell silent.

Isla took the opportunity to wipe down the crumb-splattered table with a wet cloth. Jade had to give her credit. It was the perfect moment to try to fend off wild animals.

Lauren sighed. "Look, we've got a big day ahead of us. The opening ceremony, the bonfire tonight...let's have some quiet time in our bunks."

Jade lifted her chin. That was what she had been trying to do when Miss Rage Face ripped down her sheet. "Fine."

Archer snorted. "I don't need a nap, thanks." She stomped back to the table and shoved another handful of Pringles into her mouth.

Lauren tensed as if expecting the fight to start up again. When it didn't, she picked up the lavender sheet. "Okay, then. Let's get this back in place."

Jade helped press pushpins through the fabric and into the thick pine of the bunk. Once the sheet was up, she gave Lauren a grateful smile and climbed back into bed. Her shoulders slumped the moment she was hidden, and she fell against her pillow.

"If you don't want to rest, let's go outside," she heard

Lauren say. "The schedule says there's a soccer game later, and there are some lawn games out front."

"Is there croquet?" Archer shrieked. "Challenge for master champion!"

Finally, the cabin was silent.

Crisis averted.

But deep down, Jade feared the trouble with the girls was just getting started.

Chapter Five

Isla's allergies were killing her.

It was like nature itself had conspired to turn her into a sneezing mess. The Fireflies had spent an hour out in the courtyard of their cabin cluster playing croquet, and the pine trees had put her allergies into overdrive. Now, on the walk to the soccer field, Isla tried to focus on the questions Lauren fired at them, but it was hard to concentrate; everything seemed foggy, with her itchy eyes and nose.

"You've never been to camp before, either?" Lauren asked.

"Nope." Archer shrugged. "What about you, Isla?"

"No, thank goodness." Isla swatted bugs out of her face. How could there be so many insects? This place was an entomology exhibit come to life. "My parents waited until now to torture me."

Archer burst out laughing, but Lauren looked horrified. "You don't like camp?"

Isla hesitated.

"I have an Internet business back home. I don't know how I'll manage to keep up with everything while I'm here."

Lauren's gray eyes went even wider. "Wow. You have a *business*?"

"What's it called?" Archer asked.

Isla blushed. "'What's in a Name?' I make monogrammed headbands and sell them, mostly online. My site has decent traffic."

"Monograms?" Archer grinned. "I would rather eat toenails than wear a monogram." Quickly, she added, "No offense."

"I think it sounds cool," Lauren protested.

Isla waved her hand. It was nothing compared to the accomplishments of her brothers. Carter was the valedictorian in his graduating class and had received a full ride to MIT. William was an expert rugby player and was being scouted by teams in Europe. Selling a few headbands hardly deserved praise.

Embarrassed, she changed the subject. "Lauren, you're from Arizona? I've never been out west."

The question hit the mark. Lauren launched into a detailed description, leaving Isla free to focus on not tripping on the wood-chip-covered path. All around them, huge trees stretched to the sky like the skyscrapers in New York. The path between the bushes reminded her of dark alleys—so thick with foliage, it was impossible to see what could be lurking.

If a bear leaps out, I'll wave my inhaler like a can of mace. Wait—my inhaler!

The pockets of her hopelessly unattractive camp trousers were empty. Her inhaler was still in her designer handbag back at the cabin. It was rare that she needed it, but if she did, she would need it fast.

"I have to go back." Isla felt rude interrupting a story about Lauren's parents. "I forgot something."

Lauren shielded her eyes from the sun. "We'll come with you."

Isla wanted to say yes, because walking alone through the woods felt ominous, but she didn't want her cabinmates to find out she had asthma. It made her feel like such a failure since everyone else could be active without issues. Recently, her entire family, including her grandmother, had run a marathon together. It was an accomplishment Isla couldn't even imagine.

"Thank you, no." She lifted her chin. "I don't want you to miss the soccer game."

Before the girls could protest, Isla darted down the pathway. To keep from giving in to the terror of the woods, she thought of the cute boy from the country store.

Jordan.

He had the most beautiful eyes. So dark.

Will I ever see him again?

Possible, since he attended the boys' camp across the way. Would he remember her? For a second, before she spilled the chocolate shake down her shirt, it had seemed like he couldn't stop staring at her too.

Isla was so preoccupied, she forgot Jade was still in the cabin. After climbing the wooden stairs, she pushed open the screen door. The sound of snuffles filled the room.

Was Jade crying?

Isla took a few steps, the floorboards creaking under her designer shoes. "Jade?"

Sniffle, sniffle, snuff.

Quickly, Isla shoved her inhaler into her pocket. "Sorry to bother you," she mumbled, but Jade didn't respond.

Feeling bold, Isla peeked behind the lavender sheet. Jade sat with her back facing the door while tinny music pulsed from a pair of white earbuds. She was flipping through what looked like a scrapbook, with pictures of her and another girl. Jade brushed her fingers against one of the pictures and let out a low moan. Her pain was so raw, so real, that Isla felt embarrassed.

Turning, she rushed for the door, grateful Jade had not seen her. The awkward feeling stayed with her through the forest and to the soccer field.

Lauren was in the thick of a game, running even faster than the older girls as she chased after the ball. Archer sat on the sidelines, digging into the ground with the heels of her boots. Isla picked her way through the grass and stood next to Archer, watching the game in silence.

Archer got to her feet. "You look pale. You okay?"

Isla put her hands to her cheeks. It was most likely the sunscreen. The zinc did give a ghostlike appearance to her face. That said, she felt shook up from what she'd witnessed in the cabin.

"I'm fine. Really," she added, since Archer's bright blue eyes looked skeptical. "I'm just hot. In fact, we really should drink some water. It's important to stay hydrated. We wouldn't want to get heatstroke."

Archer peered at her from beneath heavy black eyeliner. "Heatstroke?"

"It happens when you get overheated and dehydrated," Isla explained. "Eventually, your organs shut down."

There was a girl at school, Leanna, who had gotten heatstroke when her family went on safari in Africa. She had to be transported by air to a hospital in a neighboring village. The same type of thing could happen here, considering their remote location.

"Sounds painful," Archer said. "Well, the counselors have popsicles." She pointed at two girls holding clipboards and standing guard over a bright red cooler. "I bet that would cool us down faster."

There was a loud cheer as the game ended. Lauren ran over, her eyes lit up and her freckled cheeks flushed pink.

"That was so much fun," she cried.

"Good game," called another camper, tossing a fluorescent ball her way.

Lauren caught it with her knees, juggling it back and forth.

"Wow." Isla squinted. "How do you do that?"

"Here, I'll show you," Archer joked.

Lauren must have taken her seriously, because she whipped the ball at Archer's bony knees.

Archer shrieked and flailed her hands. It careened off her thigh and ricocheted off a tree, practically whacking Isla in the head. She burst into terrified giggles, which made Lauren and Archer laugh too.

"Want to go get popsicles?" Lauren asked. The other campers had already swarmed the area around the cooler.

"Yes, yes, a thousand times yes!" Archer cried.

Lauren linked her arms with Archer and then Isla. The three headed over to the popsicle line, chatting like old friends.

Lauren looked down at her bracelet. "Jade is really missing out."

"I'll eat two popsicles," Archer said. "One in her honor."

Isla giggled with Lauren and Archer as they got in line. But once the laughter died down, she couldn't get the sound of Jade crying out of her head.

Chapter Six

Archer had to admit it: camp didn't suck.

Kicking around the soccer ball and joking with the girls from her cabin was fun. Lauren was the least fake person she'd ever met, and Isla was hilarious, the way she acted like a sophisticated little grown-up. The girls of Firefly Cabin—other than Jade, of course—were nothing like what she'd expected. They were...nice.

More than that, they were normal.

It felt strange to be around normal people. Back home in Chicago, her closest friend, Wanda, spiked her hair with raw eggs and hated anything "mainstream." She almost died laughing when she learned Archer was going to camp.

She'd never talk to me again if she knew I was having fun. It would be like I had gone to the other side.

But so far, Archer really was sold.

"I cannot wait to get to this bonfire," Lauren sang as they traipsed down the main pathway. "The opening ceremony is going to be amazing!"

The Fireflies—besides Jade, who was still hiding behind her stupid sheet back at the cabin—were headed to the ceremony at the beach. The early evening air was lush with humidity and the scent of pine, and the girls who were on their second or third year sang camp songs as they walked.

Isla swatted at the air. "Ugh." Without a hint of irony, she said, "I don't think I'm wearing enough bug spray."

Archer snorted. Before they left the cabin, the girl had practically bathed in organic mosquito repellent.

"Don't worry." Lauren gave Isla a playful nudge. "If there's anything scary, I'll get it."

Scary like my sister?

Not that she could tell her new friends she was related to something worse than a killer pack of mosquitoes.

The idea of bumping into Makayla had her stomach in knots. One well-timed put-down and the Fireflies could decide Archer was a total freak. So far, she really liked these girls. She didn't want to lose them.

"I hope we don't get in trouble because Jade isn't with us," Isla said.

Lauren shrugged. "I tried to convince her."

"The cabins are supposed to sit together," Isla grumbled.

She sounded so put out that Archer nearly laughed. Archer was just happy to have friends to sit with at all.

They stepped out of the woods and onto the beach, and her boots immediately sank into the sand.

"There it is," Lauren squealed.

Archer blew a colored strand of hair out of her eyes and took everything in.

Sand as dark as brown sugar stretched for miles, speckled with rough bushes and reeds along the shore. Down to the left, a circle of wooden risers was packed with campers, surrounding a stage. Makayla, thank goodness, was nowhere to be seen.

One of the counselors stood on the beach, holding one of their ever-present clipboards. "A bright Blueberry Pine welcome! The ceremony starts at the bleachers." She pushed her sunglasses back on her head and pointed. "Once it's over, you'll go to the firepits for dinner and eat with your cabin cluster. Have fun!"

Along the lake edge, the kitchen staff set warming trays on picnic tables. The stacks of hamburger and hot dog buns made Archer's stomach growl.

"I'm starv—" she started to say, but immediately lost her appetite.

Makayla strutted into sight from the path by the risers. She tossed her hair like the star of a music video, and all the campers seemed to stop and stare. The Bluebirds followed close behind.

"Who is that?" Lauren said. "She's really pretty."

"Don't know, don't care," Archer lied, and headed toward the seats.

She climbed up the shaky wooden steps as high as she could go, and slid in. With her Sharpie, she sketched a dragon on her wrist for protection. Makayla hated dragons, ever since the Halloween when a boy dressed like one had stolen her candy, so maybe it would help her to stay far, far away.

Lauren slid in next to Archer. "This is so perfect," she breathed.

It would have been if it weren't for the looming threat of her sister.

"Hi, Fireflies!" Cassandra walked up the risers, popping a bubble with every step. "Where's Jade?"

"Uh…the bathroom," Archer lied. "She's been in and out all day." Heck, if they were going to get in trouble, they may as well have fun with it. "We're pretty grossed out, to be honest."

"Yikes." Cassandra tossed her long ponytail, braces glinting in the sunlight. "We'll need to make sure she's all right. Next time, someone should stay with her. Deal?"

Archer almost burst out laughing. "I'm sure Isla would be happy to do that."

Isla shot her a horrified look. "I most certainly would not."

"Archer," Lauren scolded as soon as Cassandra headed back down the bleachers. "Not funny." Then she added, "Okay, kinda funny. You said she was in the *bathroom*." And they both giggled uncontrollably.

"Hey, I got us off the hook," Archer said. "Besides, it's where she belongs."

Isla raised her hand as if she were in class or something. "I suspect that Jade—"

The slow pulse of drums cut through the evening air, and Lauren sat up straight, clasping her hands. "It's starting!"

The camp counselors gathered in a circle around a fire. The lead counselor threw a log onto the flames, and a burst of sparks shot into the sky. The air went thick with the scent of hickory smoke.

"Friendship!" cried a voice.

The counselors grabbed hands.

"Trust!" called another.

The group turned to the right and collapsed into one another's arms.

"Adventure!" a voice shouted.

Like acrobats, they knelt on one another's backs to form a perfect triangle. The counselor at the top lifted her arms as if reaching for the stars. The drums reached a fever pitch, and the girl on top lit a gigantic sparkler.

In the flash of light, she proclaimed, "Blueberry Pine, commence!"

The campers went wild. Feet pounded against the wooden risers, and the seats squeaked and shook like they might collapse. Just then, Archer noticed Jade standing at the bottom of the bleachers.

In the golden light of the evening, she looked mystical; like an elf or something. Like someone Archer might actually want to be friends with.

Come on. She's nothing but rude.

"Jade," Lauren called, waving like a flag.

Jade sauntered up the risers as if she were right on time. She perched next to Lauren as the president of the camp took the stage.

"Good evening. I'm Barbara Middleton, the president of the

Blueberry Pine Camp for Girls. In the tradition of Blueberry Pine excellence, we have selected one of our brightest stars to read our camp poem. Makayla McAdams, will you come up here?"

Archer sucked in a breath of hot air. "No."

Lauren glanced at her. "What is it?"

"Indigestion," Archer mumbled.

In a crystal clear, confident voice, Makayla read the Blueberry Pine induction.

> The sun stretches across the weary morn;
> Loons cry across the lake and lawn.
> Our girls are fast asleep,
> Eager for reveille as they dream.
> Music sounds, the day is here, our sleepy faces
> Light with cheer.
> Blueberry Pine has become our home;
> Lifetime friendships quickly form.
> We laugh, joke, rejoice, and sing;
> Swimming, hiking, playing games.
> Our hearts are grateful for each day.
> The light of day dims with the night
> But our campers,
> Like stars, forever shine bright.

Everyone but Archer listened with rapt attention. The moment Makayla said the last cheesy line, the audience exploded with cheers.

"That was really good," Lauren cried.

Archer tried not to gag.

Once the ceremony had ended, the counselors instructed everyone to head to the bonfires on the beach. Makayla commanded the center of the circle, and Archer felt frozen in her seat. It would be impossible to exit without walking right past her sister.

"Come on." Lauren nudged her. "I can't wait to roast hot dogs. One of the Dragonflies told me they have the ones with cheese inside."

Archer followed her cabinmates down the rickety steps, hoping to sneak past. Unfortunately, one of the counselors chose that very moment to add another log to the bonfire, and a piece of flying ash got caught in Archer's throat. She broke into a coughing fit, and her sister glanced over. A wicked smile stretched across her face.

"Is there snow in the forecast?" Makayla trilled. "That girl wore boots. Quick, someone bring me my parka!"

The Bluebirds tittered.

Archer looked down at her boots, which had seemed so cool at home. Now, they felt hot and all wrong in the summer sun. She wished she hadn't worn them, wished she wasn't such a loser, wished she had never come here at all.

"I think I just felt the first snowflake," Makayla sang.

The nearby campers also started laughing, looking up at the sky. Cheeks flaming, Archer tried to think up a decent retort but couldn't.

To her surprise, Lauren bustled forward and took her arm. Isla took her other one, and even Jade moved up to stand with the group.

"I think what you're saying is mean," Lauren told Makayla. "Please leave her alone," she said, and propelled Archer toward the exit. Once they found a space away from the crush of campers, she gave Archer a searching look.

"You okay?"

Archer looked at her feet. The thing with her sister was humiliating, but her heart was filled with a cautious optimism.

"I can't believe you did that," she admitted. "No one has ever stood up for me like that."

"Of course we're going to stand up for you." Lauren gave her a tight hug. "You're a Firefly."

Isla frowned. "I wonder why she picked on you."

"Because I was born." Everyone but Jade laughed. "No, really." Archer felt her cheeks turn red. "I…I'm her sister."

"What?" Lauren's eyes flashed. "If I had a sister, I'd never treat her like that."

"That's good to know." Archer held up the wrist with the friendship bracelet, trying to make light of the situation. "Because you're my honorary sister."

Lauren beamed. "We're *all* sisters. We're the girls of Firefly Cabin."

Everyone touched bracelets, except for Jade. She fiddled with a loose string on her shirt, looking like she'd rather be anywhere else.

Well, so what? If Jade didn't want to be friends, that was her problem. For the first time in her life, Archer had finally found her people.

Chapter Seven

Lauren was thrilled. The opening night of camp was perfect. When they got to the firepits, the kitchen staff served hamburgers, veggie burgers, and hot dogs, along with heaping sides of deliciousness like macaroni and cheese, baked beans, and watermelon.

I've never seen so much food!

Lauren followed the Fireflies to a large, available log where they could sit by the fire. The lake had gotten darker with every hour that passed, and she imagined it would turn black in the darkness. Turning, she looked at her new friends. Isla studied the bright orange bonfires across the water with interest, while Archer sat cross-legged, happily shoving mac and cheese into her mouth. Jade sat in silence, barely eating.

"What's over there?" Archer pointed across the lake.

Isla sat up straight. "The boys' camp. Blueberry Lane."

"There's a boys' camp?" Archer sounded surprised.

Lauren gave an eager nod. "I read about it on the camp website. It was founded forty years before ours. We patterned a lot of our activities after the boys, once girls were allowed to play sports and stuff."

Lauren had always been good at running and playing soccer but had never been able to participate in team sports at school due to the cost and the time. She'd signed up for every league they had at camp, including soccer, tennis, and beach volleyball. She couldn't wait to be part of a team.

Isla swatted away a mosquito. "Will we get to interact with the boys?"

"Yes." Lauren gave another enthusiastic nod. "I read these blogs from girls who have been to camp here, and they said there's usually a few events with the boys. Plus, there's a big coed dance toward the end of camp."

"Oh, wow." Isla bit into a piece of corn on the cob, eyes wide. She looked equally ecstatic and terrified at the prospect.

Archer moaned. "Boys hate me. Especially once they meet my sister."

Jade tossed her full plate of food into the fire. It sent up a flurry of sparks. Brushing sand off her legs, she stood.

"I'm going to bed."

"It's only seven o'clock," Lauren protested.

Jade stretched. "Sorry. I'm tired."

Disappointment filled Lauren's heart. She wanted to sit around the campfire and get to know the girls. If Jade went to bed, that wouldn't happen.

"Come on, Jade," Archer said. "You could give us a chance, you know."

The hint of hurt in Archer's voice surprised Lauren. Ever since the Fireflies had stood up for her in front of her sister, it was like the hard shell she had brought to camp had fallen away. Now, she had that defensive look on her face all over again.

Jade shoved her hands into her pockets. "I'll see you in the morning."

"We covered for you earlier, but we're not doing it again," Archer said.

"Tattle if you want," Jade said lightly. "But I sincerely doubt I'm not allowed to sleep." With a toss of her hair, she strolled toward the woods.

Archer stabbed a plastic fork at the air. "What is wrong with that girl?"

Why would anyone leave a campfire? It almost did seem like Jade didn't want to be at camp at all.

The fire crackled as they talked, warming Lauren's cheeks and making her hair smell like woodsmoke. Archer and Isla were by far the most interesting people she'd ever met.

For starters, Isla was from New York City and lived in a fancy apartment with a doorman. She rode an elevator every day, had two older brothers who sounded perfect, and her parents were these big-shot lawyers. Once, when her mother had worked on a case against a corrupt corporation, Isla and her brothers had taken bodyguards to school.

And Archer was apparently a really good artist. She talked about mixed media, oil painting, and drawing for at least ten minutes straight. Once they moved on to the topic of school,

Lauren learned she was also supersmart at math and science but did her best to hide her talents so the boys wouldn't make fun of her.

Lauren ached to share the story of this one foster home where the oldest boy had bullied her for getting better grades than him, but she couldn't, or the girls would know she was an orphan. It was so nice to feel normal that she only felt a little bit guilty for lying.

When the kitchen staff handed out marshmallows, chocolates, and graham crackers, Lauren watched, fascinated, as Archer stuck her stick straight into the flames. The marshmallow burned bright orange and blue, then distorted into a blackened, gooey hunk.

"Impressed by my craftsmanship?" Archer asked.

Lauren grinned. "No, I've just never roasted a marshmallow before."

The girls looked at her in shock.

"How is that possible?" Archer demanded. "Where are you from again?"

Immediately, Lauren realized her mistake. If she wanted to keep her secret, she had to be more careful. "I meant I've never *incinerated* one before."

It wasn't exactly a lie, but it did the job. Archer went back to smashing her marshmallow between graham crackers, and Isla nibbled at a chocolate bar.

Lauren slid a marshmallow onto a stick and stuck it near the fire. It started to bloat, the edges turned brown, and she pulled it out before it could catch fire. The moment it cooled, she took a bite and melted sugar oozed into her mouth.

Heaven.

Then the strangest thing happened: the forest suddenly glowed with tiny lights. They blinked and flashed, practically dancing through the night.

"What is that?" she cried.

"Fireflies." Isla's eyes got big. "I've never seen so many of them before."

All the campers fell silent, staring at the woods.

Thousands of what seemed to be white Christmas lights lit the forest, flickering and sparkling in a steady rhythm. Their energy increased, and they streaked through the dusk like shooting stars.

Magic.

"Make a wish," Isla whispered, closing her eyes.

Lauren didn't want to be greedy. This experience was more than she'd imagined. Still, she squeezed her eyes shut.

I wish for the girls of Firefly Cabin to be the best of friends.

Lauren had never had a best friend. She'd attended several schools but had never had the freedom to hang out after school or invite anyone to her house. As a result, the girls were friendly but kept their distance. Here, she finally had the chance to see what it would be like to experience that.

When she opened her eyes, the fireflies stilled.

Archer clapped. "That was epic."

Slowly, the campers returned to roasting marshmallows. The Fireflies sat in companionable silence.

"It's a shame Jade missed out on that," Lauren said after a moment.

Isla shifted in her seat. "Something happened today. With Jade."

"What?" Lauren asked, instantly worried.

Isla fiddled with her watch. It was dainty, with sparkling jewels and gold accents. "Do you remember when I returned to the cabin before the soccer game? Well, Jade was looking through a scrapbook and crying. Wailing, really. It was quite sad."

Archer frowned. "Why? What's the big deal about the scrapbook?"

Isla pushed her bangs out of her eyes. "No idea."

Archer leaped to her feet. "I'm on it."

"No," Lauren scolded. "You can't just—"

But Archer was already darting down the path.

Isla looked stricken. "Oh dear."

Lauren rubbed her hands against her legs. She didn't want to invade Jade's privacy. On the other hand…just because Jade didn't want their friendship didn't mean she didn't need it.

It didn't take long for Archer to rush back down the sand, cheeks flushed with victory. The scrapbook was tucked under her arm, and she handed it to Lauren.

"She was asleep, so it was super-easy to swipe."

Archer sat with a thump, and sand scattered around her boots.

Hands trembling, Lauren flipped open the book.

"BEST FRIENDS" hung in bubble letters over a picture of Jade and a beautiful girl with dark brown hair. The pages showed the girls' friendship from kindergarten to junior high school. There were pictures of them playing in a sandbox, celebrating birthdays, and in formal dresses with two cute guys.

Archer made a big show of yawning. "I bet they're in a fight."

Lauren bit her lip. "No. I doubt a fight would..." She flipped to the last page of the book and gasped.

There was an obituary for Jade's best friend.

The Fireflies looked at one another in horror.

"What happened?" Isla whispered.

The obituary was in both Spanish and English. Lauren skimmed the one in English, fighting to read the small print in the dim light of the fire. The opening sentence read, "Kiara Maria Flora—a smart, well-loved girl with two younger brothers and an older sister—was killed in a car crash on New Year's Eve."

"Kiara's older sister was driving," Lauren breathed. "She hit a patch of ice, spun out, and hit a tree." Pained, she touched her bracelet. "Those friendship bracelets have to be from Kiara. That's why Jade didn't want to wear mine."

Isla's eyes filled with tears.

Archer shoved her. "Don't *cry*," she said, but looked close to tears herself.

The other campers were singing "Let It Be." As the words floated through the air, Lauren's heart ached for Jade.

"We can't tell her we saw this." She shut the book. "But we have to be there for her, no matter what. Deal?"

Isla gave a firm nod, but Archer didn't respond.

She couldn't still be mad at Jade after this, could she?

"Archer, we really need to—"

"I know." She looked down at her hands. "I just feel super-guilty for acting like that earlier. But yes, of course. Jade's a Firefly. We'll be there for her, no matter what."

Lauren grabbed her hands and squeezed them. Their group sat in silence as the ash from the fire drifted away in the wind.

Chapter Eight

Jade woke with a gasp. Shadows clawed at the bunk above her, and she pulled her blanket close.

Another nightmare.

This time, she and Kiara were at that hotel their parents had taken them to in Florida. There was only one s'more left at the snack bar. Jade wanted it, so she pushed Kiara into the swimming pool, and into the jaws of a snapping shark, to get it.

If Kiara were alive, they would laugh at the idea of a shark in a swimming pool. But nothing seemed funny anymore. Especially since the last thing Kiara had said to her was "You're not my friend. You're a traitor."

If only that day had been different. If only *she* had been different.

Reaching under her pillow, she pulled out the letter she'd received earlier that afternoon and shined a flashlight on the page.

Dear Jade,

I can't believe you'll be at camp when you get this! The pool won't be the same, but I'll dunk Bobby a couple times for you. Maybe we can see a movie when you get back? You'll have to stop ignoring me at some point. LOL. Seriously, though, I hope you're making new friends and letting yourself forget about everything back home.

Have a good summer.
Your friend, Colin

Jade fiddled with the edge of the paper.

Colin was her brother's best friend. He was just a year ahead of her in school, but she'd never noticed him until her parents' Christmas party. She and Bobby had had a big group of friends over to celebrate in the basement while the adults ate appetizers and gossiped upstairs.

* * *

Kiara came over early. She looked amazing, as always. Jade felt pretty for once, too, instead of tall and awkward, in a sparkly sweaterdress and her mother's diamond earrings.

"You look like Elsa," Kiara breathed.

It was the ultimate compliment.

The party was a blast. They ate chocolates and Christmas cookies while everyone danced and told jokes. Colin made everyone laugh. For the first time, she noticed he had a great smile.

Then Kiara leaned over and whispered, "Colin is gorgeous."

So, that was that.

They had a rule that if someone called a crush on a guy, the other couldn't like him too. Jade had promised to help Kiara talk to him.

The rest of the night, Jade put them on Colin's team for group games. Even though he kidded with both of them, she thought he was watching her.

When the party ended, Colin slept over. Around one o'clock in the morning, Jade went to the kitchen for water and found him at the table, drinking a Coke and playing a game on his phone.

She pulled her nightshirt close. "What are you doing?"

"Couldn't sleep." He gave her a wicked grin. "Bobby snores, you know."

She giggled and sat with him, sharing silly stories about her brother. Before she headed back to bed, Colin whispered, "You looked beautiful tonight."

They FaceTimed every night that week. It was a delicious secret to keep from Bobby and her parents, but she felt bad hiding it from her best friend.

Jade resolved to confess everything on New Year's Eve. She and Kiara had spent it together their entire lives, dancing to the video countdowns and drinking sparkling grape juice as the ball dropped. It would be the perfect time to get her approval. Unfortunately, things didn't work out that way.

Kiara's parents had to manage the family restaurant, so she caught a ride with her sister. Cat wanted to get to a party, so as a surprise, she dropped Kiara off early, just in time for Colin's New Year's FaceTime call. Jade heard a small gasp and turned around, midsentence, to see her best friend's face turn red with betrayal.

Kiara didn't believe Jade planned to tell her. Furious, she called her older sister to come back and get her. Right before stomping out of the room, she pointed at Jade and said, "You're not my friend. You're a traitor."

That was the last time Jade ever saw her.

* * *

It was awful losing her best friend. Worse? Knowing she was the reason Kiara had been on the road at all.

The guilt and heartache had kept Jade home for months. She'd avoided her friends and ignored Colin.

One night, he came to their house for a barbecue and approached her while Bobby and her dad were arguing about the Cubs.

"I miss talking to you, Jade."

Up until then, Colin had been all jokes, like laughter could color a world without Kiara. His serious tone had made something inside her break open.

"I miss you too," she'd whispered.

His face had split into a huge smile. He'd stepped forward and panic had filled her heart.

Traitor, traitor, traitor…

"Colin, I can't." She'd darted across the lawn, her vision blurred with tears.

Ever since that stupid, weak moment, he had tried to reconnect, but she hadn't responded. Now, he'd sent this letter to camp.

Jade *did* miss him. His smile, humor, and friendship. So much of what he said made sense.

I hope you're making new friends and letting yourself forget about everything back home.

How? Kiara was supposed to be here! How could Jade make friends with the girls in her cabin with that in mind?

That's not fair, though. To them, or you.

Jade stared up at the springs on the bunk bed above her. She was so tired of being depressed all the time. Maybe Colin was right, and she needed to give the girls in her cabin a chance.

Raising herself up on one elbow, she considered the letter in her hand. His words made a difference, but that didn't mean she could write him back. She had to let him go, to make up for what she'd done to Kiara.

You're not my friend. You're a traitor.

Jade crumpled the letter into a tiny ball. From now on, his letters would go into the campfire. Maybe then her best friend's last words would finally get out of her head.

Chapter Nine

Once the Fireflies had eaten breakfast, Isla reviewed the morning schedule posted on the board in the mess hall. Swimming, canoeing, hiking…

Where was the option to go home?

It was already ninety degrees outside. The hall felt like a steam room. It was hard to breathe, and she hadn't even done anything.

What if I have an asthma attack?

It had happened at school once, during PE, before she officially had asthma. Her lungs had gotten tight, she couldn't breathe, and the gym teacher had to call an ambulance. Her parents were baffled and quick to inform the doctors that asthma did not run in the family. The next day, everyone had kept asking to hear the story. Someone like Archer would have reveled in the attention. For Isla, it was one of her most embarrassing memories.

"You ready?" Archer jogged over and whacked her back.

Isla flinched. "Please don't do that. It hurts."

"It *hurts*?" Archer snorted. "We've got to toughen you up, princess."

Princess? That's what these girls think of me?

"I am not a princess." Isla lifted her chin. "Please don't call me that."

Isla didn't want to pick a fight with Archer, but she did feel it was important to let her know what was and what was not acceptable. Ever since she was young, her parents had taught her and her brothers the importance of setting boundaries.

You show people what you are willing to accept by your words and actions, her mother always said. *So use care with both.*

"Look, I meant it as a compliment," Archer said. "Few people are true royalty. You're one of the lucky ones."

Isla let out a huff and headed outside. It felt like an oven. Plus, it smelled like dirt and moss and, ugh, nature. Almost immediately, she sneezed.

Lauren caught up to her. "You okay? Archer was just teasing."

"I know." The sun glistened beyond the canopy of pine trees. Quickly, Isla reached into her bag. "I just wanted to take the time to put on some more sunscreen. It's a spray, so I figured it would be best to do it outside."

It was an excuse, but she didn't want it to seem like Archer's comments had upset her, especially since Archer was walking toward them. Jade was right behind, looking glamorous but tired.

"Sunscreen." Lauren bit her lip. "I can't believe I forgot to pack it."

"They sell it at the canteen." Archer strolled up. "Want to go grab some?"

"Uh…" Lauren flushed. "I don't have any money on me."

"You can charge it. According to my sister, they'll just bill our parents."

"No, I...I don't want to make us late to Flagpole. I'll just grab some out of the buckets like I did yesterday."

The buckets were a cheerful green with blueberries painted on them, stationed at various locations. They held survival supplies like bug spray, sunscreen, and first aid kits. Isla hadn't seen any on the way to breakfast, and it seemed dangerous for Lauren to wait.

"Use mine." She handed Lauren a spray bottle. "You're much too fair to be in the sun without it."

"Thank you." Lauren seemed relieved. "I would have looked like a lobster by lunch."

The Fireflies walked to the common area for Flagpole, the morning meeting. Isla's thoughts were panicked. Oh how she wished she could hide in the cabin and embroider headbands. It seemed so much safer than this. The only thing that kept her going was knowing the cute boy from the store was somewhere across the lake.

Isla smoothed her thick bangs at the thought. The motion caused a bee to attack her pink nail polish, and she shrieked. Of course, Archer burst out laughing.

"Hang in there, princess," she sang. "You'll survive."

* * *

By the end of Flagpole, Isla doubted she would, in fact, survive. The meeting kicked off with a camp song that involved vigorous jumping, followed by stomping. From there, the counselors made them play some game where they had to run all around, meeting one another. Then they connected with the rest of the Insects for their first group activity—a morning hike. The group went through the forest, up the hills overlooking the lake, and back down to the shore.

By the time they were done, Isla was exhausted. The distance was not the issue. She and her mother often walked across the entire city in an afternoon. However, those hikes typically ended in an air-conditioned museum lobby or a Broadway show. The hike at camp ended with bug bites, a sweaty back, and a pinched feeling in her left foot.

The Fireflies peeled off their shoes to walk down the beach for the next group activity, a canoe trip. An enormous blister covered Isla's heel. It stung every time her skin touched the sand, and she winced.

"I'm going to have to have my mother send me another pair of shoes," she said to no one in particular, before she remembered her mother was in Europe.

"You mean a pair you didn't steal from a runway model?" Archer said.

Isla looked down at the patent leather loafers dangling from her manicured hands. Yes, they were a designer brand, but they were supposed to be functional. Besides, they looked much better with the camp uniform than Archer's ridiculous combat boots.

"I'll have her send you a pair too," Isla shot back, "since we don't appear to be under attack at the moment."

Everyone laughed, but Archer looked hurt. Immediately, Isla felt bad. It wasn't like her to be so rude.

It's the heat. You can apologize later.

But she didn't know if she wanted to. It was almost like she had to stand up for herself or get run over, which she was not used to.

"Let's go, campers!" Taylor, one of the lead counselors, stood on the beach with a bullhorn in her hand. She was a pretty African American girl with an infectious smile, and Isla was completely intimidated by her confidence. "We need to change into our suits and get into the canoes, pronto!"

Fidgeting, Isla followed the stream of campers into the large green building on the edge of the shore. The interior was lined with enormous metal lockers. Each one had the symbol for one of the cabins. The Firefly locker sat in the corner, next to one of the rickety, backless wooden benches lined up across the room.

Earlier, Cassandra had brought over their uniform swimsuits and towels. Isla grimaced to see the suits hanging in the locker together. She would have to monogram hers, because she didn't want to put on someone else's suit by accident.

That's a guaranteed way to spread germs.

"The lake might evaporate if you don't hurry up," Taylor shouted from outside. "Move it!"

Lauren laughed. "Hurry, Fireflies." She stripped off her clothes right there. Without skipping a beat, Archer and Jade did the same.

Isla gripped her suit in embarrassment. Ever since she started wearing a bra, she did not like getting undressed in front of other people. In gym class at school, she always changed in private, and back at the cabin, she'd snuck off to the bathroom. The idea of taking her clothes off in front of an entire roomful of strangers...she couldn't do it.

Before anyone could comment, Isla darted into a private stall and yanked the curtain closed. She put on her swimsuit as quickly as possible.

"Last call, campers," Taylor roared. "If you are not outside in one minute, I will personally volunteer you to sing a solo of the Blueberry Pine camp song at lunch."

That did it. Everyone dashed outside, giggling and squealing.

The campers lined up on the spongy sand, and Isla glanced down the row. The swimsuits, she had to admit, were cute. They were forest green one-pieces, in a 1950s style, with high waists and large white buttons up the front. The camp certainly was not trying to be fashionable; they had just used the style for so long that the suits were trendy again.

"All right, Insects," Taylor called. "Pick a partner. The two of you will share a canoe. We'll learn how to row, have a ten-minute practice round, and then take a rousing journey across the lake. Campers, commence!"

Instantly, Isla grabbed Lauren's arm. "Will you go with me?"

Lauren was athletic, so partnering with her seemed like the safest thing to do.

Quickly, Isla slid on one of the green life jackets the counselors were handing out. It smelled like dried seaweed, but she pulled the straps as tight as they would go. She expected the wooden paddle to be heavy enough to pull her overboard, but when she picked it up, it was surprisingly light.

Once the counselors had taken them through a quick lesson on captaining a canoe, they ordered the campers into the boats. Isla was so scared, it felt like her heart was going to beat out of her chest. What if she accidentally hit Lauren in the head with the paddle? What if it was too hard to row? Or worse, what if the canoe capsized and she got trapped underwater?

"Come on!" Lauren scrambled in, stationing herself in the middle. "I'll row. You steer."

Isla tiptoed up to the canoe. The metal stung her blister and the backs of her legs. The seat was lower than she expected, and she tumbled in, practically dropping the paddle into the water.

"Hang on," Lauren cried. "Here we go."

Isla tried to remember what the counselors had said about steering, but her mind went blank. The canoe rotated in a circle.

"Push to the right," Lauren called. "Push!"

Tentatively, Isla pushed her paddle into the water. To her surprise, the canoe came to a stop.

"Good," Lauren cheered. "Now, switch back and forth."

Isla gave an earnest nod. The paddle dripped icy water across her legs, but she didn't mind because with Lauren's instructions, the canoe actually went in the right direction. She was steering!

"Great job, Isla," Lauren sang. "Keep it up."

The encouragement gave her confidence. The counselors motioned for everyone to line up in the water. Twenty canoes jockeyed for a position in line, along with three canoes of counselors heading up the front, middle, and rear. Then the group moved out onto the water like a very long row of ducklings.

Isla and Lauren's canoe sliced through the lake, making a strange metallic sound with every small wave. Isla breathed a sigh of relief, surprised to find she was actually enjoying the ride. Steering the canoe gave her a sense of control that she hadn't felt since she arrived at camp.

First, the counselors took them along the edge of the shore, where frogs chirped from lily pads, dragonflies buzzed through the air, and turtles scuttled off logs and into the water. Then the first canoe turned to cross the lake.

Water dripped from the oars in a steady rhythm as Lauren paddled. Occasionally, it splashed Isla in the face, which actually felt good, given the heat. They were getting closer to Blueberry Lane. Isla hoped for a quick view but doubted the counselors would take them too far.

Isla began to feel tense as the counselors brought them closer and closer to the other side of the lake. Her heart started pounding as the boys' camp loomed into sight. Through the reeds, she spotted a soccer field. Groups of boys ran back and forth, sweating in the hot sun, and she wondered if Jordan was out there with them.

"Hello, gentleman!" Taylor shouted into her megaphone at the shore. "A bright Blueberry Pine welcome!"

Was he there? Would he see her?

There! It was him!!!

Isla ducked down low on the boat, letting out a little squeak.

"What?" Lauren squinted in the sun. "What happened?"

Isla covered her mouth with her hands and let out a series of hysterical giggles. Her bare feet banged against the bottom of the boat, making a metallic clank.

"What?" Lauren demanded, swatting at her with the paddle. "Tell me."

Isla dropped her hands. "I know one of the boys," she whispered. "I met him at the store."

Lauren squealed. "Show me which one!"

Reaching forward, Isla grabbed Lauren's hand. Once she was sure no one was looking, she guided Lauren's hand toward where Jordan was on the soccer field. "Him." Since she'd stopped steering, the canoe turned out from the line, heading closer to the shore.

"Isla, he's *gorgeous*," Lauren cried. "Oh, no. We're drifting. Steer."

Isla tried, but all feeling seemed to have left her arms. She was too busy thinking about the feeling of her hand pressed against his chest, along with the smell of grape Jolly Ranchers.

"His name is Jordan." She pulled at her paddle. "I think I'm in love with him."

At that very moment, he stopped dribbling the ball. Putting his hand up to shield the sun, he squinted in their direction.

"He sees us," Isla cried.

"Back in line, campers," the lead counselor roared.

"Go," Lauren screamed, giggling. "*Go!*"

Isla shoved her paddle into the thick muck at the bottom of the lake. The oar gurgled, and for a terrifying second, the canoe seemed stuck. Then the smell of muck filled the air, and the canoe shot through the water. Isla and Lauren worked the paddles, Isla's heart thundering with every stroke.

He saw me. I know he saw me.

They were halfway across the lake before she noticed she was breathing heavily and *not* wheezing. It was exhilarating. In that moment, she understood why Lauren liked sports.

Neither of them said a word as they maneuvered the canoe through the shallows and back onto shore. Lauren slid out of her life jacket. Then she turned to Isla and grinned.

"Isla Meyers," she sang. "I had no idea you had it in you."

The other campers were racing back to the green building to change for lunch. The bell at the mess hall rang out as loud as the megaphone blared. Isla tugged off her life jacket and squeezed it tight.

"Don't tell anyone," she begged, embarrassed. "Please."

The Fireflies would turn Jordan into a joke, and she didn't want that. He meant too much to her.

Lauren nodded. "Your secret is safe with me."

Archer walked up and Jade strolled past, heading straight for the building. Jade's oversized sunglasses made her look cool and removed, as if she didn't have a care in the world.

Isla's mother always said, *Appearances can be deceiving.* Maybe, in this case, she was right.

"How's Jade?" Lauren asked. "Did you guys talk about anything?"

"Weirdly, yes." Archer frowned. "We talked about painting."

"Did she mention the thing with her friend?" Lauren pressed.

Archer drained the last of her Gatorade. "Nope."

"Let's go, ladies." Taylor shooed them away.

"We had fun," Lauren said as they climbed the steps.

Isla gave a vigorous nod. "It was very educational."

Right before they walked in, Lauren poked Isla in the arm and grinned. Isla smiled, too, and her thoughts leaped back to the moment when Jordan had practically looked right at her.

What did it mean? Did he like her as much as she liked him?

Even though it felt impossible, everything in her screamed *yes*. She had to see him again.

It was the only way to know for sure.

Chapter Ten

Archer had nearly panicked at the idea of a canoe ride with Jade. She was convinced Jade would knock her overboard at the first opportunity. Instead, once they were on the water, Jade slid her sunglasses up her head and turned to face Archer.

"I'm sorry I was such a grump yesterday." Her aquamarine eyes were pained. "You must hate me."

The apology, along with the knowledge of what had happened to Jade's friend, made Archer feel super-guilty, especially considering how rude she'd been to Jade.

"N-no," she stammered. "You should hate *me*."

"Why would I hate you?" Jade slid her sunglasses back on. "You brought snacks."

From there, they started talking. Not a lot, but enough that the time together wasn't painful. Still, Archer was happy to get back to Lauren and Isla, because the three could be silly together. Jade was quiet as they giggled on the way to the mess hall, but once it came into sight, Archer's enthusiasm started to wane too.

At lunch, there would be no way to avoid Makayla.

Lauren must have noticed her distress, because she reached out and squeezed her hand. "The Fireflies have your back."

"Good. Because that's the first place she would try to stab me."

It was also good because the mess hall was exactly like the cafeteria at school: a wide-open space designed to maximize social humiliation. Granted, it was also a work of art, with large wooden beams across the ceiling, a glass wall with an incredible view of the lake, and enough long tables to seat 140 hungry campers and their nineteen counselors. But the mess hall already had a social pecking order, and the Bluebirds were clearly at the top.

Their table was smack in the center of the room, with a prime view of the stage, the food line, and the great outdoors. It would be impossible to get food without walking past them. Still, Archer did her best, squaring her shoulders and sticking between Lauren and Isla to avoid detection.

Makayla was talking to someone the first time she walked by, but once the Fireflies had packed their plates, her sister stared her down.

I'm coming for you, her mean look seemed to say. *Watch out.*

Jade gave a little snort. "Your sister needs to chill out."

"My sister is a total freak," Archer said, surprised Jade seemed to care. "Sometimes I wonder if she got left on the doorstep by aliens and my parents decided not to tell me."

Jade gave her a skeptical look. "Aliens?"

Archer ducked her head. "Yeah," she mumbled.

Great. I said something stupid and now she knows why Makayla is so mean to me.

"I wouldn't think aliens. More like the circus." Jade popped a fry into her mouth. "At least if you take into account the amount of makeup she's wearing."

The Fireflies burst out laughing.

Okay, Jade and I might never become besties. But this is definitely a start.

* * *

Lunch was over before she knew it, and it was time for all-camp swim hour.

"This is silly," Isla said as they walked back to the beach. "Didn't we just change out of our suits? They're going to be cold and wet."

"That's why we have two suits," Archer said.

Isla brushed away a mosquito. "But I don't want to get both of them dirty right away."

"Isla, what's the real issue?" Lauren asked. "It sounds like you're worried about something other than the suit."

Isla hesitated. "I thought you were supposed to take time to digest before swimming, or you could cramp up."

The Fireflies laughed.

"You'll be fine," Lauren said. "Just stay in the shallow end."

"I think I'm going to sit on the dock," she mumbled.

Archer, for one, was excited to jump into the lake. The moment the counselors blew the whistle, she raced in and belly flopped into the water. Silt went up the front of her suit. For fun, she swam up to the edge of the dock to splash Isla, who didn't even have her feet in the water.

"Quit it!" Isla shrieked, smoothing her thick bangs.

"It's a thousand degrees," Archer pointed out. "Don't sit up there getting fried. Get in."

Lauren splashed around with the Cicadas. Even Jade was sunbathing. Isla just sat there like a stone, sweating profusely.

"I am perfectly comfortable, thank you," she said, which was obviously a lie.

Archer sighed. There were moments when it was hard to talk to Isla, because the poor girl seemed scared of everything. Strange, considering she came from such a big city, but— Wait, that was it! Isla would be the first to know what to do if someone mugged them, but when faced with mosquitoes and fresh air, she didn't have a clue.

I can help her. Show her there's nothing to be scared of in the lake.

Archer let out a resolute breath. "One day you'll thank me for this, princess." Grabbing Isla's legs, she pulled her into the water.

Isla sputtered and shrieked, arms flailing. She threw a big handful of water at Archer. Then she raced for the shore, clutching her dripping sun hat to her head like a shield.

The reaction was so over-the-top that Archer couldn't help but laugh.

"That was not nice," Lauren scolded, swimming over to the dock. "Isla, are you all right?"

Isla stomped back to her spot without responding. She wrapped a towel tightly around her body, flopped down, and glared at Archer. Even though her face was lined with fury, it was definitely less sunburned.

"I don't know why she's so mad." Archer floated on her back, relishing the feel of the cool water against her skin. "It feels great in here." Flipping over, she spotted her sister, and her stomach dropped. "Dark mass warning. My sister is at two o'clock."

Makayla and the Bluebirds strutted across the sand, set down their beach bags, and waded in. They all dove in at once and swam out to the dive raft, just beyond the swim boundaries. Cassandra had explained it was off-limits to campers ages twelve and under. Makayla climbed to the highest board, posed, and did a perfect jackknife.

"Uggh." Archer groaned. "I can't stand her. We should do something."

Lauren giggled. "Hmm. Like what?"

"Prank her," Jade drawled from under her sun hat. "Put a rubber snake on her towel. There were tons of them on that creepy 'Take a Look at Nature' display by the changing room."

Wow, Jade didn't say much, but when she did, it was shaping up to be pretty entertaining.

"Be right back." Archer darted out of the water.

The "Take a Look at Nature" display was, indeed, creepy. It was a plexiglass table set up beneath the overhang of the green building, showcasing an entire array of the various spiders, snakes, and insects common to northern Michigan. Archer lifted the lid of the display case to grab one of the snakes, cringing at how rubbery it felt in her hand. With a furtive look at the raft, she headed back to the water, and on the way, slipped the snake into her sister's sandals.

"Did anyone notice?" she asked, once she'd slid back into her spot by the dock.

Talk about a bold move. If Makayla caught her, it would be an all-out war.

"Nope." Lauren shrugged. "They're all too busy diving."

Archer spent the next hour splashing around, excited to see the prank play out. When the Bluebirds finally swam toward shore, she flagged down Lauren, who was playing water dodge-ball with some of the other girls. She came right over.

"What's up?" she asked, then spotted the Bluebirds. "Oh boy. It's time for the fireworks." She grabbed an inner tube and floated on the water.

Archer started to feel panicked. "I think I should go to the changing room or something."

What am I thinking, doing something like this?

"No, stay here," Lauren insisted. "It's more suspicious if you leave."

They migrated over to the deep end of the dock. Jade was still sunbathing, but not Isla. She had waded into the shallow end and was slowly making her way out toward them.

Good. I've already helped her feel brave in the water.

The thought made Archer feel less scared of her sister.

Turning, she watched as Makayla made it to shore. The moment the Bluebirds reached for their towels, an ear-piercing scream cut across the lake. Makayla whipped her sandals across the beach, terror on her pretty face. There was chaos as the lifeguards and counselors ran over. It took everything not to crumple into giggles—even Jade's sun hat bounced up and down as she laughed.

There was a lot of hand waving and pointing. Then the counselor for the Bluebirds stomped away, carrying the rubber snake. Makayla sat on the dock, sipping a bottle of ice water from a lifeguard, with a towel over her shoulders and her friends hovering around her as tight as a tourniquet.

Lauren slid out of her inner tube. "I'm going to go 'find out what happened.'"

Isla had almost waded out to them when Lauren came bounding back. She had a huge grin on her freckled face. Jade dove in and swam over to them, eyebrows raised.

"What's the verdict?" she asked.

"Makayla thinks some boy with a crush snuck over to prank her," Lauren sang, her red hair hanging around her face in wet strings.

"Phew." Archer felt like she could breathe again. "Wow, she's an idiot."

Quietly, she reenacted the moment Makayla found the snake. The Fireflies hid their giggles. She was just about to suggest they all have a handstand competition when— *WHOOSH!*—she got slammed in the face by a tidal wave.

"*That's* for pulling me in the water," a tiny voice cried.

BAM!

Another wave hit.

"That's for getting my bangs wet!"

The other Fireflies screamed with laughter.

Archer opened her blurry eyes and—*WHOOSH!*

"*That's* for calling me 'princess'!" Isla roared.

Archer wiped water off her face, in complete disbelief.

This is the thanks I get?

Archer drew back to give Isla her own face full of water when strong arms gripped her from behind. Lauren and Jade had her pinned.

"Hey," she cried, kicking furiously. "You guys!"

"I believe we're girls," Jade said.

"Lauren," Archer pleaded. Surely the nice one in their group would have some mercy. "Don't do this."

"You started it," Lauren crowed. "Isla?"

Isla stepped forward with a crazed look in her eyes. She placed both hands over the top of Archer's head. The last thing Archer heard before Isla pushed her under was the glug of water in her ears and the shrieking laughter of her new friends.

Chapter Eleven

Lauren went to bed happily exhausted each night. Even after three days at camp, though, she still got up at five every morning, the same time she woke for kitchen duty at Shady Acres. It was like some invisible alarm clock seemed determined to remind her that Blueberry Pine was not real life.

Live it up, it seemed to say, *but don't get too comfortable.*

Lauren pulled the blankets up to her chin and stared at the ceiling. Camp was so perfect. Too perfect.

It was everything she'd pictured and more, but with every day that passed, Lauren realized how different she was from the other girls.

The Fireflies were amazing, but gosh, were they privileged. Every single one of them had a real home with a family, and they had unlimited resources. Archer's family could easily pay for two kids to go to camp, and her sister had been to Blueberry Pine the last three years. Isla's shirts were made of silk, and every piece of clothing she had, even her underwear, was monogrammed. Plus, they all talked about iPhones, trips to Disney World, private ski instructions, dance classes, and piano lessons like those experiences were a given.

They would be shocked if they saw my life back home.

Really, living in Shady Acres wasn't too different from camp. Lauren shared a room with five other girls and slept in a bunk bed with a thin mattress and hard pillow. Her area was decorated with pictures ripped out of discarded travel magazines, and her space in the closet held a few outfits from the thrift shop, carefully maintained so they would last.

It could be worse. Based on some of the things she had experienced in foster care, it could be a lot worse. Sometimes, though, she wished it could be so much better.

Lauren looked out the window, at the tall pine trees draped in early morning mist. It was so beautiful. Pushing the negative thoughts out of her head, she decided to get up and walk around the lake.

Outside, the air was wet with humidity, and the birds called to one another. She followed the hiking path the girls had taken that first day. In the silence, her thoughts turned to Jade.

That's someone who doesn't have it so great.

Lauren knew the pain of losing someone close to her. Not her parents—they died when she was three, so she barely remembered them. The one loss she remembered was the foster family she had lived with when she was seven.

The mother, Marianne, was perfect. She had two little boys and called Lauren her "precious girl." They baked cookies together and fed ducks in the park, and each morning before she left for work, Marianne braided Lauren's hair. For a brief, hopeful moment, there was talk about adoption—until the factory where Marianne and her husband worked closed.

With barely enough money to survive, Marianne had tried to make it work, but there were too many hungry nights. When Lauren went back into the system, she was so heartbroken she didn't speak for months. That experience taught her not to get attached to anyone, because everyone left in the end.

It was hard to watch Jade learn that lesson too. Lauren wished she knew how to help her.

She walked for more than an hour, thinking about her new friends and taking in the scenery. Around six thirty, she headed back, passing by the kitchen on the way.

Smoke billowed out of the chimney, and the aroma of powdered sugar and bacon lingered in the air. Lauren's stomach growled. Creeping to the back door, she peered through the screen.

Cinnamon donuts were cooling on racks on the counter. They had to be for the campers, but it wasn't breakfast yet. Lauren was about to turn away when a firm hand clamped down on her shoulder.

"Don't even think about it," growled a voice.

Lauren jumped. Turning, she came face-to-face with a plump, freckle-faced woman with hair as red as hers, but streaked with gray. The lines in her face were tight with anger, and her voice had a hint of an Irish brogue.

"You trying to steal my donuts, you little thief?" the woman demanded.

Lauren's face went hot with indignation.

"I'm not a thief." Lauren's voice shook. "Don't call me that."

The chef scoffed. "I'll call you whatever I like. You spoiled brats think you can take whatever you want? I'll tell your counselor and you'll get a one-way ticket home."

"No," she cried. "Don't send me home!"

The threat was terrifying, especially when she'd worked so hard to get here. Before Lauren could stop herself, tears rolled down her cheeks. Embarrassed, she turned to face the dirty wood of the building.

"Hey." The chef sounded surprised. "Come on, now." She took Lauren by the shoulder and guided her through the opened screen door. "Sit." She patted a stool by a counter and poured Lauren a glass of water.

"I wasn't going to take anything." Lauren's words came in short bursts. "Please don't send me home."

"I was only teasing." She patted Lauren's arm. "Now, calm down."

Lauren let out a deep breath. Jazz crackled from a radio in the kitchen, the smell of cinnamon hung thick in the air, and finally, the tears stopped. Ashamed, she got to her feet.

The chef's expression was much kinder than before. "Better?"

Lauren hugged her arms to her chest and nodded, watching the woman transfer the donuts into a metal warming tray.

"I'd thought you were homesick, getting up this early."

"Habit," Lauren said, her voice dull. "I get up at five every day at home to help out in the kitchen." The chef gave her a funny look. "I should get back."

"Wait. You can't leave here empty-handed."

To Lauren's absolute shock, the chef ambled over to the cupboard and pulled out a large bag. She packed it with a dozen donuts, boiled eggs from the refrigerator, cartons of milk, and apples. Then she placed it into Lauren's arms.

Chef smiled. "Now, don't start telling people you got this from me."

"Oh thank you." Lauren leaped forward and gave her a hug, the brown bag rattling between them. "Thank you, thank you, *thank you*."

Chef moved away and turned to the stove. "Go on, now." She waved her hand as if shooing a fly. "I'm not going to waste all day with you."

In spite of the gruff tone, Lauren was certain she saw Chef smile.

Chapter Twelve

Jade had just climbed out of bed when Cassandra returned to the cabin. She'd left right after reveille for a meeting with the counselors. The other Fireflies were camped out at the table in their pajamas, food spread out like a picnic.

"Hey, Cassandra," Archer said. "Could you please tell Isla eating in the cabin won't attract bears?"

Jade grinned. Lauren had started bringing back donuts after her walk each morning, and ever since, Isla had been cleaning up cinnamon sugar like it was her job. She'd spent the past few mornings armed with wet paper towels, swiping at every crumb.

"Gosh." Cassandra made a clucking sound. "I can't really say that, because you've heard about Ainsley O'Neill, right?"

Everyone stopped and looked at her.

"Ainsley was one of the counselors last year. One night, her campers snuck in s'mores. A bear broke in, ate every marshmallow, and dragged Ainsley away by her socks. It was really quite sad."

Isla's eyes were as big as donut holes. "That's awful."

"Welcome to the food chain." Cassandra beckoned to Jade, who had just finished dressing. "Hey, can you come with me for a minute? I need to talk to you about something."

On the way out the door, Isla could be heard saying, "We need to get this food out of here, now. That's awful, what happened to that girl!"

Cassandra grinned at Jade. "I'll tell her the truth later," she said, and stopped just below the cabin steps.

The morning was already hot and muggy. Next door, the Butterflies were having a hula-hoop competition.

"So, it's Friday," Cassandra said, as if that explained everything. "I need to escort you to the infirmary for your appointment."

Jade gave her a blank look. "Appointment?"

"Your parents signed you up for counseling sessions."

"Counseling sessions? For what?" Jade demanded.

"They don't tell me that, doll." Cassandra glanced at her clipboard like the answer might be there. "They probably figured you had some things on your mind and might want to talk to someone."

Seriously?! Why do adults think talking makes a difference?

Kiara wasn't coming back. All the chatter in the world wouldn't change that.

"Can I just skip, please?" Jade muttered, swatting away a mosquito.

"Unfortunately, no." Cassandra gave her a sympathetic look. "I hear Mrs. Anderson's really nice, though."

Jade pulled her arms close. She was so thin, her body didn't feel like her own. "What am I supposed to tell the girls?"

"Some campers pretend they have a weekly phone call with their parents."

I won't talk. I'll sit there in silence and look out the window at the trees.

If there was a window. There probably wouldn't be, for "privacy."

"You ready?" Cassandra said.

"When will I be back?" Jade demanded.

"In time for Flagpole," Cassandra said. "The girls will never know you were gone."

Yeah, right. So much for trying to be normal and make friends. Jade felt the overwhelming urge to crawl back into bed.

"Ready to go?" Cassandra asked, again.

Jade shoved her hands into her pockets. "Whatever."

When had her life turned into such a nightmare?

* * *

Jade rushed toward the main courtyard, trying to make it on time to Flagpole. She tugged at her corduroy trousers, already wet with sweat from the early morning humidity.

The meeting with the therapist was exactly what she had pictured. The lady was fine, with a tired perm and friendly face, but she actually expected Jade to start talking about her friendship with Kiara.

Hello, she wanted to say. *That's never going to happen.*

Talking about it hurt, and she was tired of hurting. Tired

of the nightmares, the guilt, and the fact that all the talking in the world wouldn't bring her best friend back.

Jade came to a stop on the main lawn. Campers were clustered around the flagpole, chatting and giggling. Like always, the Bluebirds had taken the only spot in the shade.

The very sight of Makayla irritated her. It was obvious the younger campers idolized her, and in Jade's opinion, that came with a certain level of responsibility. The fact that Makayla used her popularity to humiliate her sister, hog the spotlight, and create an environment of exclusivity was not right. Power was a privilege, and Makayla did not have the first clue how to handle it.

"Jade," Lauren called, waving.

The Fireflies turned her way. They looked relieved to see her; like maybe they'd thought she'd gotten sent home or something. Jade strolled up and faced the flagpole, as if she'd been there the whole time.

"Ready, girls?" shouted Taylor into her bullhorn.

Immediately, the campers launched into the Blueberry Pine camp song.

"Friendship is precious, friendship is *true*…"

Archer made a gagging face, like she always did, and Jade nearly did too. The words to the camp song were not what she wanted to hear each morning. They glorified friendship and how it lasted forever, which was a total lie.

It doesn't last forever, she wanted to shout. *It could be over tomorrow!*

What would everyone think of her then?

Once the horrific song was over, Taylor led everyone in the Pledge of Allegiance. Then she gave them a big smile. "Before we discuss the activities of the day, I have exciting news to share."

"Blueberry Pine is about to be coed," Archer cracked.

Isla let out a frightened squeak.

"She's kidding," Lauren assured her.

"The camp's marketing materials—the website and brochure—have been the same for nearly a decade. The board has decided to update everything, so they are proposing a contest: the Faces of Blueberry Pine."

Archer raised an eyebrow. "Ooh. Do you think it's about redesigning the site?"

Jade shrugged, surprised to discover that she and Archer shared another interest. Web design used to be one of Jade's passions. Of course, she hadn't wanted to spend any time on it in months.

"Over the next few weeks, each cabin will compete in a series of events," Taylor continued. "The cabin that earns the most points in the competition will become the new face of Blueberry Pine, and its members will be featured on the website and on the front cover of the Blueberry Pine camp brochure."

The campers erupted. Everyone—including Lauren and Isla—jumped up and down like idiots. But Jade just fidgeted with her friendship bracelets, wondering if anyone would notice if she snuck back to the cabin for a nap. The competition was the type of thing that, once upon a time, she would have been determined to win, but now, the prospect sounded exhausting.

Lauren—ever the optimist—turned to them, eyes shining.

"I have looked at the website and brochure thousands of times," she squealed. "I would love to be the face of Blueberry Pine with all of you!"

"Don't get your hopes up." Archer picked a scab from a mosquito bite, sounding as depressed as Jade felt. "Clearly they want my stupid sister to model. It's a conspiracy."

Taylor hit the siren on the bullhorn. "Ladies. Listen up."

The chatter died down.

"We'll post the series of upcoming events following lunch, but the first one will start today, as our activity of the morning. Each cabin is challenged to create a visual depiction of your cabin name. For example"—the counselor pointed at Makayla and her friends—"the Bluebirds might transform their cabin into a giant bird's nest."

Yikes. Maybe Archer is onto something. The counselors do seem to have their eyes on the Bluebirds, which is completely unfair.

"Use anything you can find," Taylor continued. "Cabins will be judged by a team of counselors before lunch. The first-, second-, and third-place teams will receive points toward the competition, which will be tracked on a board throughout the contest in the mess hall. Good luck, and happy decorating!"

"We can win this," Lauren insisted. "It's the perfect way to remember this summer forever."

"I don't *want* to remember this summer," Jade said, without thinking.

The Fireflies looked at her. Immediately, Lauren's face flashed with...pity? Impossible. No one knew.

Jade slid on her sunglasses. Kiara used to call them her celebrity shades, since they practically covered her face.

Lauren put a hand on her arm. "Was everything okay this morning?"

"My parents can only call on Fridays." She felt momentarily grateful to Cassandra for the quick excuse. "Look, if you want to win this, we should start. I have an idea."

Jade didn't want to participate, but she also didn't want to keep letting down the Fireflies. There wasn't much she could do about not wanting to hang out, share secrets, or wear the Firefly bracelet; she really wasn't up for that. But she did have a good idea of what they could do for the contest. It wouldn't hurt to pass it along.

Lauren clapped her hands. "Huddle up!" Once the Fireflies were in a close circle, she gave Jade an expectant look. "What is it?"

"The forest at night," Jade suggested. "You could black out the windows, hang some stuff from the ceiling made out of foil so they look like flowers—like moonflowers. Then you could blink flashlights or something. To represent fireflies."

Lauren put her hand to her mouth. "Oooh."

Isla gave an eager nod. "That's beautiful."

Even Archer looked impressed.

"You know what?" Jade added, starting to feel inspired. "Isla has that noise machine she sleeps with. Doesn't it do crickets or something?"

Isla nodded. "Crickets, waves, and wind."

The look on Lauren's face almost made Jade laugh. It was like Lauren couldn't believe anyone would spend money on something that mimicked the sounds right outside the window. Archer must have felt the same, because she *did* laugh.

"Princess comes through yet again! How about white Christmas lights for the fireflies? I accidentally walked into a storage room at the Lodge, and there were boxes and boxes filled with holiday stuff. One of the counselors shooed me out and locked it, so it's probably still locked, but it's there."

"I have a friend in the kitchen." Lauren brushed a bead of sweat off her forehead. "I can ask her for some foil to make the flowers, and maybe she'll have a master key too."

"I want to black out the windows," Archer said. "I've done it in my bedroom. I drew a bunch of stuff on the walls in this glow-in-the-dark ink…it's really cool."

It sounded cool, actually, and Jade half wished they had something like that to use for the night forest.

"What did you black out the windows with?" she asked. "Please don't say Sharpies, because I doubt the counselors would go for that."

"Black tarps," Archer said. "Isn't drama an elective? The theater would have some lying around."

Lauren looked at her digital watch. "Come with me, first,

to get the foil to start the flowers and explain where we can find the lights. We have two hours. Let's do this!"

Then she stuck her hand out as if they were football players or something. Archer and Isla put their hands on top of hers. Jade hesitated, but it seemed easier to put her hand in the circle than try to fight it.

Lauren fluttered her hand. "Zzzap, zzzap, zzzap!"

The other girls laughed. "Zzzap, zzzap, zzzap," they cried, bouncing their hands in return.

Their voices became louder and louder. Then everyone lifted their hands in a burst of cheers and applause.

"We have a secret handshake," Lauren cried. "Let's do this!"

Lauren, Archer, and Isla's enthusiasm was contagious. For the first time since camp started, Jade felt like she was a part of things. What surprised her even more was that she actually wanted to be.

Chapter Thirteen

Isla could barely catch her breath. Lauren dragged them to the kitchen without stopping once to rest. The morning was especially humid, and her lungs felt thick. She leaned against the stone edge of the building, sweat soaking her silk shirt.

"Hey, you okay?" Jade looked at her with concern.

Isla nodded. "Mmm."

She was not about to admit the truth.

Jazz music wailed through the shabby screen door, and Lauren gave a firm knock. A hefty, frizzy-haired woman came to the door, a look of thunder on her face. Her expression softened at the sight of them.

"So, missy." She wiped the sweat off her forehead with an apron. "You need more donuts already?"

"No, ma'am. I need your help." She explained about the contest while Isla fought to catch her breath.

The chef let out a dramatic sigh. "Is there a reason you enjoy bugging me?"

Lauren grinned. "I'm not trying to bug you. We knew the

kitchen would have foil. And when my friends asked who would have a key, I told them if anyone would, it would be you."

The chef looked flattered. "Well, then." She wiped her hands on her apron. "I suppose I can help you. The camp rents out the Lodge for parties during the year, so I imagine all that stuff should be fine for you to use."

"Jackpot," Archer said.

Jade nodded, sliding her friendship bracelets up and down her arm.

Chef returned with a huge roll of foil and a set of keys.

Archer and Jade headed off with the foil, while Lauren and Isla followed Chef to the Lodge. The trail leading to it was empty, with late-morning patches of sun dancing on the ground.

The air-conditioning inside helped Isla's breathing. She sank onto a sofa, relieved, as Chef unlocked office doors. Finally, she found the room Archer had described.

"Mum's the word," Chef said. "Lock the door behind you."

Lauren leaped forward as if to hug her, but the chef waved her off. "Go on, now." She waddled away. "Mum's the word."

Lauren grinned. "Mum's the word."

Isla followed Lauren into the room and stopped short. There were stacks of clear bins filled with decorations— Halloween, Easter, Fourth of July...and there! Christmas.

Lauren put on a Santa hat and pulled out a string of white Christmas lights. She dropped a Santa hat on Isla's head too. For a second, Isla was concerned about contracting head lice, but since Lauren didn't seem worried, she tried to have fun with it.

"How do you know that lady that let us in?" Isla asked. "The chef?"

Lauren explained some incident with donuts. "She threatened to send me home." Her shoulders hunched at the memory. "I was really scared."

"I would have been too."

Isla never felt brave enough to talk to authority figures. Some of the girls at camp were already making friends with the counselors, which seemed so bold. The counselors were all in college, and Isla didn't have the first clue of what to say to them.

"You like it here, then?" Isla took her hat off and traced her hand over the faux fur.

"You still don't?" Lauren flopped onto the floor and crossed her legs. "Is it because of your business?"

Isla hesitated. She wished she could tell Lauren how hard things had been and that she struggled to keep up every day. The risk was too great, though, that Lauren would think she was a baby.

People like winners, her father liked to lecture. *Not whiners.*

"I like it." Isla folded the hat. "It's just an adjustment."

"How do you mean?"

Isla fidgeted. Lauren had a way of looking at her, really looking, as though she wanted to hear what Isla had to say. She was so different from the girls at private school.

"I've never spent time in the country. The whole princess thing..." She waved her hand. "Archer is right."

Lauren sighed. "I'll ask her to stop calling you that if it bothers—"

Isla shook her head. "It's funny. I just wish…" She bit her lip. "My brothers are so successful at everything. They went to camp at Blueberry Lane, and like everything else, they dominated it. Their words, not mine. My parents expect me to do the same, but I don't know how to be successful at…nature. I wake up every day scared I'm going to fail."

"Oh, honey." Lauren pulled her into a hug. "No one fails at *camp*."

Isla gave a muffled laugh against her shoulder. "I could."

"Look, if you fail here, it's still a win because it doesn't matter in the slightest. No one will ever know. Besides, you're not going to think about canoeing or swimming once this is all over. You're going to think about the friends you made. That's what matters. You know?"

Such great advice. Isla nodded, but felt embarrassed that she'd shared so much.

They gathered up the Christmas lights, and Lauren locked the doors behind them.

"We should hurry." Lauren glanced at her digital watch. "We don't have much time."

Here we go.

Lauren started to run and Isla forced herself to keep up. They raced through camp, holding the lights to their chests. Isla's lungs ached with the effort, but she managed.

They approached a cluster of bird cabins, and Lauren

came to a halt and pointed. "Look."

Somehow, the Swans had found an enormous, blow-up swan. It sat on their front porch, surrounded by a bunch of faux, sparkling snow that glistened in the sunlight.

"Wow," Lauren marveled. "That looks so cool."

Isla's heart pounded with nerves. Would their entry be good enough?

There you go again. Trying to overachieve.

This was different, though. The Faces of Blueberry Pine competition was important to Lauren. Isla wanted to do well because it meant so much to her. She made a silent vow to do everything possible to help. That proved difficult, however, when they returned to Firefly cabin and the door was locked.

Lauren banged on it. "You guys! Come on."

They heard a telltale pair of combat boots stomp across the floor.

"Who is it?" Archer sounded suspicious from behind the door.

Lauren giggled. "Who do you think?"

Archer undid the latch and let them in. "Hurry. The other cabins are trying to spy."

"We need your help making flowers," Jade said immediately. "Everyone, grab a piece of foil and copy our prototype."

The only light came from the fluorescents buzzing overhead, since the two had successfully found tarps and blacked out the windows. The prototype flower was easy to follow, and Isla enjoyed the opportunity to craft, rather than run all over the place. Jade gathered the flowers as quickly as they could be made and hung them from the ceiling with the assistance of a small stepladder.

"Okay, I think this is good. What do you girls think?"

Isla had been so focused on making flowers that the sight of the cabin caught her by surprise.

"Wow," she breathed, looking around.

Firefly Cabin felt like a different world. Whimsical flowers and foil-covered streamers hung from the ceiling like something out of a moonlit dream. Her sound machine chirped in the background, creating the sense of a forest at night.

"It looks…" Lauren spun around, taking it all in.

"Amazing," Isla said.

Quickly, the Fireflies worked together to tack up the white Christmas lights. Lauren held the plug next to the outlet. "Drumroll, please."

Archer banged her fists against the wall and stomped her boots. Jade tapped her fingers against the edge of a bunk, and Isla held her breath in excitement. Suddenly, five hundred shimmering Christmas lights lit the small cabin, reflecting off the silver flowers.

"Yes." Jade gave a firm nod. "I knew it would work."

Lauren clasped her hands. "It's absolutely perfect."

"It *is* perfect." Isla pointed at the clock. "But it's almost noon."

The moment the words left her lips she regretted them, because the Fireflies let out a yelp and tore out of the cabin.

They raced down the wooden path to the main lawn. Isla did her best to keep up, but after a morning of exertion, faded fast.

Lauren turned to beckon at her. "We can't be late or we're disqualified."

Isla's entire body burned with the effort. Sweat poured down her back, her legs ached, and her lungs got tighter with every step. A telltale whistle started to take over. Somehow, she made it to the main lawn, but it was too late—she was in the thick of an asthma attack.

Ducking behind a pine tree, she pulled out her inhaler and pressed it between her lips. She felt light-headed as the sharp medicine shot into her lungs. The grip on her chest loosened and she could breathe.

Archer rushed behind the tree, her face like thunder. "What are you *doing*?"

Through the branches, Isla could see Cassandra marching toward the Fireflies. Lauren looked absolutely panicked.

Isla rushed past Archer to join the others. The girls stood in nervous silence as Cassandra checked them in.

Once their counselor had walked away, Archer tossed up her arms in exasperation. "What was that, princess?"

Everyone stared at her. Even Jade.

Isla's cheeks flushed with embarrassment. "I—I thought I saw a bear. My mistake. Cassandra told me that bears wouldn't come on camp without a major food shortage." *I should just go home. Fake an illness and get out of here.*

"I would have run too," Archer said. "But next time, you need to warn us so I can trip one of you and escape."

She pretended to shove Lauren, who made a silly face, and the girls burst out laughing.

Isla looked down at her shiny shoes, hiding a smile.

Maybe she'd stick around for a while, after all.

The cheerful mood faded the longer the Fireflies stood in the courtyard, waiting for the judges. No one spoke, not even Lauren.

"Winning isn't everything," Isla said, as much to herself as anyone. "We should be proud of how good our cabin looks, no matter what happens."

"Speak for yourself." Archer cracked her knuckles. "I want to beat my sister."

The counselors returned with the verdict, and the Fireflies—even Jade—grabbed hands. The judges handed Taylor the paper. She opened it, read the results, and gave a perky nod.

"The third-place honor goes to the Crabapples."

The ten-year-old girls jumped up and down, shrieking in delight.

"Second place goes to…" Taylor pointed at Makayla. "The Bluebirds!"

"Gag," Archer cried. "This is so rigged!"

Makayla leaned against the oak tree, as if posing for the brochure. She didn't look happy, though. Perhaps because the Bluebirds weren't first, which meant maybe…

Isla's stomach tensed as Taylor squinted down at the paper.

"First place goes to the girls of Firefly Cabin," she cried. "We'll tally your points and put them on the board during Indoor Rec. Everyone, thanks for participating. The cabins look awesome."

Isla couldn't believe it. They'd won first place! Out of *all* the other cabins.

The Fireflies bounced up and down, cheering and hugging one another. Lauren's face flushed with pride, Archer shot victorious looks at her sister, and for once, even Jade was smiling. They gathered into a huddle, grinning from ear to ear.

"We're going to be the faces of Blueberry Pine," Lauren squealed. "I can feel it! Bring it in."

Every single one of the Fireflies brought their hands in for the secret handshake.

"Zap, zap, zap," the girls cried.

Giggling hysterically, they headed back to their (first-place!) cabin.

Chapter Fourteen

It was pretty awesome walking into lunch as the first-place winners. The daggers the Bluebirds shot at the Fireflies made Archer giggle. It would be amazing if she and the Fireflies actually won the whole thing.

The counselors had set up a display for the contest in the entryway. It had a detailed explanation of the point system and the main competitions. These events were worth the most points, but it was also possible to earn twenty points each for doing silly stuff like switching cabins for the night, sending a letter of appreciation to a counselor, or writing a funny poem about Blueberry Pine to read aloud at lunch.

"The main ones are worth one hundred points each," Lauren squealed. "We are so far ahead of almost everyone!"

"Well, what are the main ones?" Archer said, reading down the list.

- Dress Your Cabin (already aced it)
- Stand Up, Sing Out (ack)
- The Ultimate Scavenger Hunt (could be fun)

- Rowdy Relay Race (double ack)
- The Power of the Pen Essay Competition (hard to tell)

Biting her lip, she said, "I don't know. We'll have to do some serious plotting to keep the lead."

Like everyone else in the mess hall, the Fireflies spent lunch planning how to do each and every one of the silly tasks. It all sounded like a lot of fun. Especially if it meant beating her sister again.

Lunch and swim hour seemed to fly by, and the Fireflies met up with the Cicadas to head over to Indoor Rec.

"I think I'm going to get a pass to go to the art building today," Archer said. Art was technically her Monday, Wednesday, and Friday elective, but she wanted to get back to work on the painting she'd started. "Anyone want to come?"

The art building was two buildings over. It was packed with canvases, oil paints, watercolors, pastels…basically an artist's dream. Plus, there was little chance Makayla would go there, which was an added bonus.

The Cicadas shook their heads.

"I'll go," Jade volunteered. "I've been wanting to check it out."

Immediately, Archer felt nervous. She and Jade had gotten along great while decorating the cabin, but they still didn't have that comfort level she shared with the other girls. It would be impossible to say no, though.

"Let's go," Archer said brightly.

The only sound as they walked to the art building was the crunch of Archer's boots on the path. She considered a bunch of conversation starters, but Jade seemed perfectly happy to walk in silence. Finally, Archer stopped worrying about it and let the birds chatter for them.

The screen door creaked as they walked in.

The counselor in charge, Rochelle, waved them back to the main room with the art supplies. Floor-to-ceiling windows overlooked the lake, and a line of easels waited. In the corner, a group of younger girls took a lesson on watercolors.

Archer smiled at them, then headed to the cupboard for a smock. Jade followed.

"This is where you get your supplies," Archer told her, breaking the silence.

There were several mason jars filled with paintbrushes in different sizes. Each jar sat next to tubes of the primary colors, as well as black and white, and a small board to mix them on. Archer's current canvas stood upright in a cubby labeled "Guinevere."

"Guinevere, huh?" Jade grinned. "Hiding from your sister?"

"Um…" Archer did not expect Jade to be that perceptive. "Yeah. She'd mess with it if she knew it was mine, so it's not mine."

"That's smart. Kiara and I used code names to pass notes—" She stopped suddenly, as though surprised to have said her friend's name out loud. Turning, she grabbed a mason jar and headed to an easel in the corner.

The two worked in silence. It didn't take long to forget about Jade and focus on her piece, *Firefly Cabin at Sunset.* Today, she had planned to do the sky, so she mixed up burnt red, mustard tones, and a sultry violet.

Long rays of sun stretched across the wooden floor. Archer breathed in the scent of old wood, the linseed smell of the oil paints, and Jade's rose perfume. Once the younger girls had left, the room fell silent.

"Kiara was my best friend," Jade said abruptly. "She died in January."

Archer almost dropped her paintbrush.

Wait. She's talking about this? To me?

"What happened?" Archer dared to ask.

It made her feel like a total jerk to act like she didn't know, but what could she say? *Yes, I know, because I snooped in your things the very first night we were here?*

"Car accident." Jade's voice was small. "It was kind of my fault." She added snow to a painting of a polar bear.

Huh? Kiara's sister was driving. How could it be Jade's fault?

"What hap—" she started to ask, but Jade waved her hand.

"I don't want to talk about it."

Archer bit down on the handle of her paintbrush. "You wouldn't have brought it up if you didn't want to talk about it."

"Drop it, okay?" Jade shoved her brush into the black paint and turned her polar bear into a gray blob.

"Fine," Archer said. "I wouldn't mind hearing about what she was like, though."

Jade gave a weighted sigh. Then she said, "Kiara was born exactly one month after me. We did everything together. I told her everything. Well, almost everything." For a scary moment, it looked like Jade might burst into tears. "We signed up for camp together."

Archer winced. No wonder the girl didn't want to be here.

"I bet she would have been a good Firefly," Archer said.

That made Jade smile. "Yeah. I bet you're right."

Setting down her brush, Jade leaned against the wall of windows and slid to the floor. The collar of her shirt was flipped up, and the tip of her perfect nose, sunburned. The girl looked like a Tommy Hilfiger ad—not someone struggling with a problem like this.

"You have an iPhone here," Jade said.

Archer jumped. "How did you—?"

"It lit up in your pocket the other day. Are you addicted or something? Kiara used to be obsessed with this one dumb game."

"I'm playing a prank on someone," Archer admitted.

"Your sister?"

Archer slid down next to Jade. "Yeah." She fiddled with the laces on her boots.

"Why do you hate her so much?" Jade asked. "I don't like her, and she's totally rude to you, but isn't that, like, her job as a sister?"

Archer didn't discuss this with other people. But for some reason, she said, "Because...summer break, about two years ago, she transformed into this *thing*. She started piling on makeup, talked my mom into a superexpensive haircut with highlights, and made friends with the snobby crowd. She started treating me like something that crawled up out of the sewer."

Jade frowned. "So, she became this whole new person? That actually makes sense. She's trying to figure out how to be that person. From everything I can see, she seems super-insecure."

There were times it seemed that way, but it hardly justified Makayla's rotten behavior.

"What's the prank?" Jade asked, when Archer didn't respond.

When Archer told her, Jade looked horrified.

Archer had dreamed up "Paolo" the year before, the day Makayla humiliated her in front of the entire school. Archer had just walked into the cafeteria and was standing by the door, looking for a place to sit down, when Makayla had dumped blue slime down the front of her shirt. Archer had shrieked and tripped, and she'd busted her lip on a table. The lunch monitor had yelled at her to be more careful, as if the fact that she was covered in blood and blue goo was her fault.

Archer had gone straight to her room when she got home and found a picture of a hot guy on Google. One just a little older than them, so Makayla would fall for her plan. Then she sent her sister a series of messages from Paolo, a "male model from New York."

It was hilarious, at first.

Makayla had written flirty messages, and Archer had said outrageous things back. But something unexpected had happened—her sister started taking it seriously. She'd dumped the guy she'd been talking to and bragged to everyone about her fabulous new boyfriend who traveled the world modeling and was up for a leading role in a new television series.

The situation gave Archer power, but it also gave her this weird glimpse into Makayla's world. It was messed up, but Paolo helped her know what was going on in her sister's head. It would be sad when they broke up.

It would also be the ultimate revenge.

Every time Makayla was mean, Archer thought about the breakup. She wanted it to be public, humiliating, and educational—to teach her sister not to treat other people like garbage.

"That's *awful*," Jade said. "How would you feel if someone did that to you?"

Archer jumped to her feet. "You'd better not rat me out!"

Makayla would *kill* her. Plus, it would be over. Paolo was fake, but the conversations with her sister were real. She needed them. Like that one time when Makayla had told Paolo that sometimes she felt like an outsider.

There are days I move through my life saying and doing the things people expect, like lines from a movie. I wonder, is this really me? Or am I a total fraud?

The words spoke to Archer's deepest fears. There had been so many times she felt the exact same way, like a total fraud. Like when Cotton Candy Baby Doll's latest music video came out, Archer had made fun of it because the girls who hated

Archer loved the video. But that night, alone in her room, she'd watched it ten times in a row, dancing and mouthing along with the words.

I know what you mean, she wrote back to her sister. Most days, I live in this box people have put me in. They would be shocked to know what I really thought and felt!

Her sister had replied ten minutes later. ☺ Finally. Someone who understands me.

"Girls," Rochelle called back to them. "It's about time to get back to your group for capture the flag."

"I know how to keep a secret." Jade got to her feet. "But what you're doing isn't right."

The two put away their supplies in silence. Jade dumped her painting into the recycle area. Outside, the sky had gotten dark, as if it might rain.

Jade looked at her. "I'm not judging you. I just want you to think it through." Her blue eyes were pained. "It's easy to make assumptions about someone based on how they look, but you never know what people are going through. Do you know what I mean?"

Archer looked down at her boots. "I'm sorry to hear about your friend."

Jade shoved her hands in her pockets. "Yeah. Me too."

Chapter Fifteen

It rained for three days straight.

Jade didn't mind. She liked falling asleep to the lightning that flashed just outside the window, the rich smell of the damp earth in the forest, and the raindrops glistening on the screen. She also liked the fact that the camp had all these indoor activities like movies and scavenger hunts that weren't mandatory, so she could spend as much time as she needed napping in her bunk.

Lauren got on her for it, though. "I understand that you're tired," she lectured the afternoon Jade opted to sleep instead of attending an indoor carnival. "But you missed out on something truly extraordinary. Jade, they had a man on stilts and a live tiger. How could you sleep through that?"

Jade was groggy, fresh out of a nap. "A live tiger?"

The other Fireflies burst out laughing.

"Dang it, you guys," Lauren cried. "I almost had her." Then Lauren passed a cone full of blue cotton candy into her bunk. "You were there in spirit."

Jade ate it in one sitting and actually joined the girls for a game of cards.

The only drawback to the time indoors was that it gave Archer's sister way too much time to pick on her. The latest incident happened during Indoor Rec, when the rain outside poured down like a deluge.

The Fireflies had been seated around a long table, gathering supplies to decorate picture frames, when one of the Cardinals walked over. She set down a picture torn from a magazine.

"This is from a secret admirer," she said, then walked away.

Eagerly, Isla grabbed it. "That's weird. It's a dog with blue and purple hair."

Moments later, another camper walked up. "Candy-gram," she sang.

This time, it was a picture of a pig with blue and purple hair rolling around in mud. The Fireflies all seemed to get the significance at once. They turned to look at Archer.

Archer did a great job pretending she didn't care, but Jade could tell she was embarrassed. The whole tough-girl thing was clearly an act. Jade knew Archer well enough already to get that she was supersensitive, no matter how much she tried to hide it.

Jade held up her hand as another girl approached. "Stop right there. What do you want?"

The girl hesitated. Then she looked across the room.

Jade followed her gaze. Makayla sat at a corner table with the Bluebirds, gesturing at the girl to continue.

"I think you dropped this," the girl mumbled, and placed another picture on the table.

It was a donkey with its bottom facing forward and his head turned to look over his shoulder, showcasing a big-toothed grin. Of course, he had blue and purple hair.

The Bluebirds shrieked with laughter. Rage shot through Jade. She was about to tell the girl what she could do with the picture when Lauren beat her to it.

She shot to her feet, face red with fury. "You leave my friend alone," she hissed. "Or I will take a glue gun to your hair."

The girl screamed and darted away. Lauren stood at the edge of the table, fists clenched like she might still go after her anyway.

Their counselor rushed over. "Everything okay?" Cassandra asked, resting her hands on the art table.

Archer slid the pictures under her project. "Fine."

Jade nodded. "We're good."

Cassandra gave a perky nod, then headed back to gossip with the other counselors in the television area.

Lauren sank into a chair. "Sorry. I didn't mean to get us in trouble."

Rain drummed against the roof. The crowded room was getting hot, and Jade looked over at Makayla. Their eyes locked. After flashing a catlike smile, Makayla turned back to her friends.

"Your sister really needs to back off." Jade twisted her ponytail. "We need to do something."

"Like what?" Lauren asked.

"Prank her," Isla suggested, taking a drink from her water bottle.

Jade nearly choked. "What?"

"Prank her. I found the thing with the snake quite funny." She stuck a flower decal to the corner of her picture frame. "Why not do something similar?"

Jade loved that a prank sounded innocent when it came from Isla. The Fireflies really were starting to grow on her.

"You know..." Jade flexed her fingers. "I have a good one. If you're interested."

The Fireflies leaned in.

"Someone could sneak into their cabin at night," she said. "Draw a pink heart on everyone's forehead except Makayla's. Then plant the pink Sharpie on her pillow. The Bluebirds would totally blame her."

Lauren's freckled face split into a grin. "Where do you come up with this stuff?"

"Eh." Jade squinted at her picture frame. "I used to be a lot of fun."

The girls fell silent, and rain continued to pound against the roof in earnest.

"I believe that." Lauren's voice became gentle. "What changed?"

Jade drew back. Lauren's tone indicated she knew exactly what had changed. That meant Archer was a two-faced rat.

"You know what, Archer?" Jade speared her with a look. "You suck."

Archer's face crumpled, and Jade realized her mistake.

"Wow." Archer's heavily lined eyes filled with tears. "First, my sister treats me like crap, and now you. I should have expected it. Thanks."

Jade opened her mouth to speak, but couldn't. Instead, she rushed away from the table and searched for the door. It was too hot, there were too many people, and she had no business being around any of them.

She was a terrible friend.

* * *

Outside, Jade stood beneath the overhang of the door. The rain was coming down too fast for her to run out into the yard without getting soaked. Tears streamed down her face, and her breath came in ragged gasps.

Why didn't I trust Archer? I really am a terrible, terrible friend.
She put her hands to her ears to drown out the words.

"Hey." She felt a hand on her arm. "Jade. Talk to me."

Lauren stood there, her red hair frizzy around her worried face. She was such a nice person. She didn't deserve to be around a monster like Jade.

"Leave me alone!" Jade rushed down the steps and into the rain. She raced to the enormous weeping willow down by the lake and stared out at the water, shivering.

It was all so gray. Like how she felt inside.

What if I dove in? And never came out?

A chill rushed through her, followed by a warm hand gripping her arm. Lauren. Her hair hung in wet strings, and her upper lip trembled. "I am *not* going to leave you alone! You're my friend."

"You don't want to be my friend," Jade cried. "Let me tell you what happens when I'm your friend."

In short, angry bursts, she told Lauren about the night of the wreck. Her stomach twisted with the memory. When she repeated Kiara's final words, she expected Lauren to draw back. Instead, she pulled Jade into a tight hug.

"Let me go." Jade pushed at Lauren, who hugged her even tighter.

"No," she whispered. "Kiara would not want you to feel this way."

When the therapist said that, Jade had scoffed. Hearing the words from Lauren made them feel authentic somehow. But that still didn't change what had happened.

Jade wrenched away. The wind whipped the branches of the weeping willow tree, slapping her in the face. "Please leave me alone."

"Let me help," Lauren pleaded.

"*How?* Kiara is gone because of me. Can you change that?"

"No." Lauren's face was fierce. "But you would if you could. Right?"

"Of course," Jade cried. "I would have gotten in the car instead."

Lauren's eyes filled with tears. "Then how are you a terrible friend?"

Lightning lit the sky. Thunder crashed and someone

shouted from the porch. Cassandra waved at them with a furious expression on her face.

Lauren looked back and forth between their counselor and Jade. "I know this isn't easy, but I don't want you to forget this summer. You're a Firefly, Jade. Nothing will ever change that."

Jade's throat tightened. She was so tired of being alone, battling this on her own. Would it be so terrible to let someone in?

Cassandra shouted once again. Then she started to stomp down the porch steps.

"Shoot!" Lauren burst into giggles. "We'd better go."

Lauren grabbed her arm, and Jade ducked her head. They fought through the rain back to the building, where Lauren tried to tell Cassandra some convoluted story about seeing a rainbow.

"I don't want to hear it." Cassandra handed them ancient Blueberry Pine sweatpants and sweatshirts. "Go get dry."

"Let's go," Lauren said, holding up the clothes.

"Okay." Jade hesitated. "Then there's something I need to do."

Nothing had changed. She didn't deserve good friends. Still, the second she put on dry clothes, she took a deep breath and went to apologize to Archer.

* * *

Jade found Archer sitting alone in one of the Lodge's storage rooms. Her eyeliner was smudged but still thick, like she'd cried for a second, then made herself stop. She scrambled to her feet when Jade opened the door.

"Excuse me." Archer tried to force her way out.

"Archer." Jade put her hand on her arm. "Can I please talk to you for a second?"

"Why?" Archer's expression was a million different shades of hurt. "So you can tell me again how much I suck? I already know that, thanks."

"I'm so sorry. I..." Jade glanced at the open door. "Can I please shut this?"

Archer hesitated but finally moved aside. Crossing her arms, she glared. "What do you want?"

"You do not suck," Jade said. "You're awesome, Archer. You're so authentic, which is why I told you about Kiara in the first place. I thought, if anyone would have something real to say, it would be you. And I was right. The things you said about her being a good Firefly..." She choked up. "It meant a lot to me. But I'm not used to sharing secrets with people other than her, and when I thought you told Lauren, I panicked. I'm sorry." When Archer didn't say anything, she slid down to the floor and sat in silence for a minute. In a low voice, she said, "The thing is, I'm not great at being a friend these days. I've made too many mistakes, and really, I don't think I deserve good friends at all. But I'd be really sad to lose you too."

Archer looked down at her feet.

"I'm not a good friend, either," she said in a low tone. "I can't keep lying to you about that."

Jade paused. Had she read the situation wrong? Had Archer, in fact, told the other Fireflies her secret after all?

"What do you mean?" she asked.

"I knew about Kiara. We all did."

Jade winced. "How?"

Did the counselors know? Did they say something?

"That first night..." Archer let out a weighted breath. "I stole your scrapbook. At the time, I thought I was being funny. I didn't realize..."

Jade flushed hot and then cold. "You looked at my scrapbook? That book means everything to me! It's—" Through the lump in her throat, she couldn't explain that the book was the only way to have Kiara here, at camp. But Kiara wasn't here, and never would be, which made her burst into tears.

"Jade, I'm so sorry." Archer slid down next to her on the floor. "If I could go back in time and change it, I would."

Go back in time.

Change it.

"There's no going back," Jade told her. "That's the thing."

"But we can move forward," Archer said. "If you want to."

Archer fiddled with her bracelet, and the firefly seemed to flash in the light. Jade leaned her head against the wall. Finally, she nodded.

Archer reached over and took her hand. Jade squeezed it. The two sat in silence, the sound of the rain pounding steady and sure on the roof above them.

Chapter Sixteen

Lauren was reading in her bunk when the rain stopped. She set down her book and sat up straight.

"Fireflies." Lauren held her breath. "Listen. It's not raining."

Isla set down the headband she had been embroidering, and Archer hid something under her blanket. Jade had taken down the lavender sheet, and Lauren watched as she propped herself up on one elbow, listening.

"It's not raining," Lauren repeated, leaping to the floor. She spun in a circle, her long hair swirling like a streamer. "It's not raining!"

Archer leaped out of bed and raced to the porch, followed by Isla's more cautious steps. In the faded light of the evening, small drips of water fell from the eaves. The forest was quiet, and the air, fresh and clean.

It didn't take long for the other cabins to catch on. Girls shouted from porch to porch, singing songs and doing funny chants. The three of them quickly joined in.

Jade walked out onto the porch and stood at the railing next to them.

Lauren smiled at her. It was such a relief to have everything with Jade out in the open. The four of them had talked late into the night, and Jade had reassured them again and again that she forgave them for snooping in her scrapbook. Then she'd shared funny stories about Kiara, like the pranks they loved to pull in school. Once, Jade had spent all her birthday money from her grandmother to have pizzas delivered every hour to the PE teacher who said girls shouldn't eat as much as boys. Jade was finally opening up and letting the Fireflies get to know her, and it made Lauren feel guilty for not being honest with her friends.

It's okay. They don't need to know everything.

Lauren pressed her thumb into a raindrop on the railing. What would happen if she told them the truth? Nothing good; she had already told too many lies.

The Fireflies wouldn't see her as their leader anymore. They would see her as someone to pity. Besides, she didn't owe them anything. The Fireflies would only be a memory once camp ended.

"Hey, look," Isla said in her tiny voice.

"Whoa," Archer breathed.

Like that first night, the forest was lit with fireflies. There were hundreds, if not thousands of them, flashing with a golden glow. It seemed like they, too, wanted to celebrate the end of the rain.

Pushing all the negative thoughts out of her mind, Lauren clasped her hands. "This is poetry," she whispered. "It's magic. It's…"

"Nauseating," Archer cracked, and everyone laughed.

Smiling, Lauren turned and faced her friends. "Make jokes if you want, but I think they're performing just for us."

"I want to paint that," Jade said.

Archer hit the railing. "That's why we're friends! You think exactly like I do."

Blueberry Pine, where the day is pure and bright

Time to sing songs and celebrate the night…

The Butterflies shouted the start of a camp song, and quickly, the other cabins joined in.

Lauren linked arms with Isla and then Jade, who did the same with Archer. The group swayed back and forth, singing as loud as they could as they stood at the railing and watched the fireflies perform.

* * *

Lauren was in an especially good mood because they had seen the points board for the Faces of Blueberry Pine competition, and so far, they were crushing the other cabins. They had done all sorts of bonus points activities while it rained and were already up to 280 points. The Bluebirds were close behind, but even they only had 240.

"It's cause for celebration," she said to no one in particular.

The forest smelled rich with damp pine and wild mush-rooms. In the stillness, the trees creaked in the wind. Looking up at the sky, Lauren came up with the most daring idea for a celebration she'd ever had.

Should I even suggest it? We could get in so much trouble.

Cassandra always left the cabin to go hang out with the other counselors until the eleven o'clock bed check. It would be easy. Besides, it would be something the girls would never forget.

Back at the cabin, Lauren waited until lights were out and Cassandra's footsteps had walked down the wooden path. Then she sat up in her bunk.

"Fireflies," she whispered. "I have a wonderful, terrible idea."

In the dark, she heard the other girls shift in their beds.

"Spill it," Archer said.

Clenching her fists, she squealed, "Let's sneak out and go for a night swim!"

The only sound was the crickets chirping outside until Archer snorted with laughter.

"I'm in," she said. "We have an hour until bed check."

"Maybe more," Lauren said. "The counselors are still in the middle of a Netflix marathon because of the rain. I heard them talking about it."

A flashlight lit under Archer's chin. Her head seemed to float in the top bunk like a ghoul. "Let's get wild."

"What about snakes?" Isla whispered. "Several species are nocturnal."

Lauren made silly hissing noises. "You only live once."

* * *

The night was spectacular. A full moon hung over the lake like a glowing mirror. The girls hushed one another as they crept down the path.

Once they reached the beach, Lauren slipped off her sandals and slid her feet into the sand. She glanced at the forest and paused.

"Let's go down farther. This is too close to camp."

The girls scampered down the shore like thieves. The spongy, cold sand squished between her toes as she stared up at the moon. The lake lapped against the shore in a slow, gentle rhythm.

Lauren stopped walking about thirty feet past the main swim area. "How about here?"

The other Fireflies nodded.

She rushed for the water and splashed in, gasping as the icy water soaked through her tank top and shorts. She waded out until she couldn't touch the bottom. In one smooth motion, she flipped onto her back.

The haunting echo of the water pulsed in her ears as the stars sparkled overhead. Mosquitoes buzzed in a high-pitched drone, and she brushed them away, diving below the surface. For fun, she opened her eyes. Complete blackness. Once she'd surfaced, the other Fireflies bobbed next to her.

"This is epic," Archer said. "I've always wanted to do this."

Isla gave a little shriek. "Something bit me," she cried, kicking away from them.

The other Fireflies shushed her, and Archer towed her back to the group.

"Nothing bit you," she scolded. "If we get caught because you acted like a princess, I'm going to put a snake in your bed for real."

"Try it," Isla muttered, and Lauren giggled.

Lauren stretched her arms out, as if embracing the night. "This is amazing."

"Totally," Archer agreed. "Just like the Fireflies. I...I never thought I would have friends like you."

"Aw," Lauren said, touched. She felt exactly the same way.

"I mean it." In the moonlight, Archer looked sad. "It's bad at school, you know? I've got this one friend, and she's just...I don't know. She hates everything. It gets old."

What would they say if they knew? That I've never even had a close friend?

"My friends are okay." Isla's wet hair clung to her head, making her look even younger than usual. "It's different here, though. I know we've only been at camp for a week, so maybe this is silly, but I feel like...I don't know. Like we're family."

Lauren's heart leaped. "I feel that way too!"

"I never thought I'd have three best friends." Archer looked at Jade. "I know you already have a best friend. I still consider you one of mine, though."

Jade stuck out her chin, her eyes damp with tears. "Thanks," she whispered.

One by one, the Fireflies grabbed hands until they floated in the water like a giant octopus.

Lauren felt joy bubble up inside. *This* was the type of friendship she'd imagined when she wrote her essay. Now here she was, living out her dream.

"Stop!" Isla said suddenly, slapping at Archer's arm. "It's not funny."

Archer looked confused. "I didn't do anything."

Jade gave a small shriek. "Stop kicking my foot, Archer. Seriously!"

Archer's eyes widened. "You guys. *I didn't do anything.*"

Lauren didn't know what to believe. Then she felt a nibble on her toes. She didn't know if it was a fish, a snake, or the Loch Ness monster, but she did not want to find out.

She swam to shore as fast as she could. The other Fireflies were right behind her. They raced out of the water and collapsed onto the shore, laughing hysterically and shushing one another with every other breath.

The giggles subsided and Lauren stretched out in the soft sand. She stared up at the sky. The starlight twinkled like fireflies.

This is everything. I want it to last forever.

The thought stunned her. Quickly, reality set in.

It can't *last forever. Nothing does.*

But the thought of saying goodbye suddenly didn't seem simple. It seemed downright sad.

Chapter Seventeen

The fact that the girls stayed up until eleven nearly every night that week did not stop reveille from blasting at seven a.m. Isla turned up the waves on her sound machine and pulled her pillow over her ears. It made no difference. The bugle was relentless.

Shouldn't there be a camp-wide sleep-in day?

That would certainly help. The late nights had started with the Fireflies sneaking out for a night swim, followed by Wednesday's camp-wide Guitar and Ghost Stories Bonfire. Then last night, the Insect leaders had taken their clusters to the beach to watch a meteor shower. The Fireflies had stayed awake talking and giggling long past the time they should have been in bed, and now, Isla was exhausted.

Can a person die from lack of sleep?

"The Lady of Shalott," a mournful poem first introduced to her by her English tutor, flickered through her mind. She imagined Jordan discovering her limp, exhausted body in a canoe. He'd drag her out, wailing, and press his lips to—

"Get up, get up, get up!"

Isla's eyes shot open.

Lauren held out a warm, cinnamon donut. "Appetizer?"

Isla hesitated. It had been days since Lauren had started bringing them donuts in the morning, and Isla had yet to spot a bear, mouse, or even an ant. The camp most likely had a system to keep them out. Plus, the donuts smelled so darn good.

"Okay." Isla caved, taking it.

"I want one too," Cassandra called, sitting up in her cot. With a wink, she added, "You girls owe me for cutting short my beauty sleep."

The Fireflies kept the chatter to a minimum on the walk to breakfast. In spite of the silence, Isla felt close to the other girls and proud of herself for everything she'd accomplished that week. It had been scary, breaking the rules for the night swim and then going out so late at night to stargaze, but instead of worrying about getting kicked out of camp, drowning in the lake, or being attacked by bats on the nightly walks through the forest, she had said yes to the adventures.

The knowledge put a skip in her step on the way to Flagpole. She put her full attention into the Pledge of Allegiance and even whispered along with the friendship song. Then Taylor pulled out the bullhorn.

"Before our daily activities," she roared, "we have an important announcement!"

Isla stood up straight. The coed dance? It was all she could think about, ever since Lauren had mentioned it.

"It's time for another event in the Faces of Blueberry Pine competition...a singing contest, Stand Up, Sing Out!"

Oh dear. Not this.

The Fireflies cheered, and Isla shifted in her loafers. Singing was her secret gift, but she was not about to share that piece of information with the girls.

"Next Saturday, you'll perform in front of a very special group of judges: the boys of Blueberry Lane. Afterward, we'll join them on the beach for a bonfire celebration."

The trees spun above Isla's head. She would finally get to be near Jordan. But why oh why did it have to start with a singing competition?

Of course, it was all the Fireflies could talk about during their nature scavenger hunt. Isla fell behind, pretending to focus on the things they were supposed to find (a flat gray stone, a wildflower, a pine cone) as the Fireflies plotted their attack.

"I used to be the captain of the dance team," Jade said. "We could do a routine to go with our song."

Dancing. Ugh.

Isla imagined falling flat on her face. It would be a repeat of the moment she'd dumped the chocolate shake down the front of her shirt. Jordan would think she was the most ridiculous human alive.

By lunch, she'd pretty much decided to give up Jordan, become critically injured, and go home, when Archer rushed to the table. Her face looked like thunder.

"We're doomed." She sank into a chair.

"What do you mean?" Lauren asked. "And where's your lunch?"

It was macaroni-and-cheese day, one of Isla's favorite meals. She'd miss it if she went home, not to mention the Fireflies.

I'd also never see Jordan again.

Perhaps leaving wasn't the solution.

"I can't eat," Archer moaned. "I've lost my appetite."

Jade frowned. "What did your sister do now?"

Archer kicked her boots against the table, jostling everyone's drinks. "My sister and the Bluebirds are outside practicing for the singing competition. My eyes are burning."

Lauren giggled. "Shouldn't it be your ears?"

"My eyes," Archer insisted. "Their dance routine is so scandalous. The boys will love the Bluebirds."

Jordan might fall in love with Archer's sister?

The very thought was horrific.

"We have to do something," Archer decided.

"Like what?" Lauren took a quick bite of macaroni. "It's not like any of us can sing."

Isla must have flinched or something, because Lauren looked right at her.

"Wait. Isla, can you?"

Oh dear. It would be wrong to lie.

"I've won a few singing competitions," she mumbled.

The Fireflies stared at her.

"A few singing *competitions*?" Archer echoed.

Ugh. Was camp invented to torture her?

Isla took a sip of water. "For chorale group at school. I also sang at the Kennedy Center. However," she added, because the Fireflies were practically bouncing up and down with glee, "I was with a huge group of people."

Archer scoffed. "So, your choir wins competitions, princess." She popped a noodle into her mouth. "That won't do us any good."

Isla paused. Something about Archer pushed Isla to prove herself again and again. Perhaps because Archer was bold in a way Isla wasn't, or because she insisted on teasing her. Whatever the reason, Isla was not about to let her minimize an area where she had true talent.

"Not the choir." Her tone was firm. "*Me*. I won three solos at the state-level competition. The choir was backup."

"Okay, Miss Thing." Archer grinned. "I think it's time to hear you sing."

Isla squeezed her hands together. Not good. The other Fireflies would force her to lead the singing competition. Terrifying, but better than allowing Jordan to fall into the vortex of Makayla's dance.

"Fine." She picked up her fork. "Finish lunch, and then we'll go to the main bathrooms, for the echo. And you can't look at me while I sing. I hate that."

"Who knew we had such a diva in our midst?" Archer cracked.

Then she burst out laughing with her ridiculous, staccato laugh. Everyone started giggling.

"Make fun of me if you want," Isla said. "I think you'll be surprised."

With that, she focused on eating as the other Fireflies watched with amusement. She got up to put her tray away. Breezing back by the table, she pointed at the clock: 11:55.

"The offer expires at noon."

Lauren, Archer, and Jade leaped to their feet and followed her to the bathroom.

Chapter Eighteen

Jade stood on the porch, staring out at the trees. The leaves rustled in the wind. It was such a pretty day.

It should have been a fun day too. The girls had worked all afternoon rehearsing their dance routine. It had taken them hours to perfect it, because they needed to incorporate a sheet that could hide Isla while she sang. Apparently, she experienced severe anxiety every time she performed in front of an audience and felt more comfortable hidden. The Fireflies finally aced using the sheet, but every shared giggle with the girls, every silly moment, reminded her of all the times she and Kiara had prepped for dance team down in Kiara's basement, until they could have done the routines in their sleep.

It made Jade miss her more than ever.

The screen door creaked and Archer walked outside.

"Hey." She gave a casual wave and settled into one of the rocking chairs.

The smell of Sharpie filled the air, which meant Archer was hard at work on another arm drawing. Through the window, she could hear Lauren telling a funny story about her brother, which made her think of her brother and Colin.

"You okay?" Archer asked.

She squeezed the wooden railing. "Sure."

The big bonfire at the beach was in an hour. She had time for a nap but couldn't get one important fact out of her mind.

"Today's Kiara's birthday."

Saying the words out loud filled her with relief. She'd sat on them all day, trying to convince herself it wasn't a big deal.

"Today?" Archer said.

"Yeah."

"Oh."

The words were short. Her communication with Archer was similar to the shorthand she shared with Kiara. It felt like a betrayal, somehow. Turning, she moved to go inside.

"Hey." Archer got to her feet. "Let's do a memorial for her on the beach. Read one of her favorite poems?"

When Jade didn't answer, Archer flushed. "Maybe that's stupid."

It wasn't stupid. It just made the whole thing more real than Jade wanted to admit. That was why she hadn't gone to Kiara's funeral.

She regretted that. She wished she'd been there to see the people fill the church (standing room only), to see Kiara's sister (and claim responsibility), and of course, to see the face of her best friend one last time.

"I'd like that," Jade whispered. "If you don't mind."

Archer nodded. "Let's grab the girls."

* * *

Jade stood by the water in silence, her friends by her side. Down the beach, the other campers laughed and sang as they arrived at the bonfire. The scent of burning wood hung heavy in the air and the sun reflected rays of gold across the water.

Archer looked at her. "Ready?"

Jade nodded. "Yes."

"Thank you for coming tonight," Lauren said, as if speaking to a large crowd. "We are here to honor the memory of Kiara Maria Flora. Her life was taken too quickly, but she made a lasting impression with her sense of humor, carefree spirit, and commitment to friendship."

A perfect description.

Archer took a step forward. "I know Kiara was an amazing person, because she had the honor of being Jade's best friend."

Jade dragged her foot through the sand, fighting her emotions. She pictured Kiara sitting on the large log by the shore, with her legs stretched out, a big grin on her face. "Shall we light the candles?" Lauren asked.

Isla's grip on a package of white, waxy candles tightened. "I don't know," she fretted. "Do we really want to be responsible for starting a forest fire?"

"We're on the *sand*." Archer snatched them away. "It will be fine."

Lauren lit a match, then carefully passed three candles around.

"Jade, did you have a poem you wanted to read in her honor?" Archer asked.

Jade clutched the piece of paper in her hand. It was warm and slightly damp from the sweat on her hands. In a shaky voice, she read the words to "I Wandered Lonely as a Cloud" by William Wordsworth, the poem Kiara had recited in English class last December.

> I wandered lonely as a cloud
> That floats on high o'er vales and hills,
> When all at once I saw a crowd,
> A host, of golden daffodils;
> Beside the lake, beneath the trees,
> Fluttering and dancing in the breeze.

The words reminded her of the way Kiara had stood in front of the class, so confident. Their classmates had listened, rapt, as she recited the poem. Now, Jade finished reading, and the words faded into the stillness of the evening.

"Let's hold hands," Lauren said, "and send our well-wishes to Kiara's spirit."

Jade wanted to tell Kiara how much she missed her and loved her. The moment she closed her eyes, though, she could only see the betrayal on Kiara's face.

Traitor, traitor, traitor...

The leaves rustled in a sudden gust of wind. Jade opened her eyes in time to see the candles blow out. Her arms prickled. If Kiara were present, Jade was afraid to face her.

"Let's go," she said quickly.

The Fireflies walked to the group bonfire in silence.

Lauren kept smiling at her, like they'd accomplished something wonderful.

Let her think that.

In truth, Jade felt sick inside.

The other girls skipped across the sand, eager to grab plates for dinner. Jade stopped to stare at the twisting flames, too numb to see anything.

Traitor.

With a trembling hand, she wadded up the poem and dropped it into the fire.

Chapter Nineteen

The night before the competition, Archer and the other Fireflies practiced their routine for hours at the Lodge. It was a relief to finally call it quits and walk out into the mellow heat of the evening. Her week had been busy with fun electives like the ropes course, skateboarding, and comic book drawing, so dancing and singing was a total snoozefest. However, it was easy to stay fired up when she reminded herself why they were doing it: to crush her sister like a bug.

Isla had an amazing voice. She sounded like a professional. It was going to be a thrill to make a stand against the Bluebirds with Isla on the mic.

As they walked onto the main lawn, Lauren came to a screeching halt.

"Hey," Archer giggled, smacking into her. "What are you—" The sentence died on her lips.

Speaking of.

The Bluebirds were practicing their dance, showing off their routine to anyone who would watch. They looked like something off a televised talent show, with their sparkly sequined rompers, heavy makeup, and tanned legs. The campers watching seemed to love it, which was beyond annoying.

"Oh, look. It's the Firebugs." Makayla hit the stop button on her MP3 player and glared. "Are you guys here to spy on us? I wouldn't be surprised."

Lauren looked confused. "Spy?"

The other Bluebirds crossed their arms and stood next to Makayla.

"Everyone knows the only reason you're so far ahead is because you're cheating." Makayla's blue sequins flashed with every word. "So, don't even try to copy our routine."

Lauren's face flushed. "Why would we copy you? We have our own routine."

"You'd copy us because you're cheaters," Makayla scoffed. "I heard you guys should have been disqualified from the cabin decorating contest. You weren't back by noon."

Isla looked stricken. "Y-yes, we were," she stuttered. "It was close, but—"

Jade stepped forward. "Hold up. We would have been disqualified on the spot if we were late, but we weren't. So nice try, but stop spreading rumors. We won because our cabin looked better than yours. It's that simple."

Makayla's blue eyes turned to ice. "Watch your back."

"Have a good night," Lauren called, and practically dragged the other Fireflies toward the woods. "Sorry, I had to get us out of there."

"I'm glad you did." Jade yanked at a branch of pine needles. "I'm so mad right now. I can't believe she'd try to get people to think we should have been disqualified!"

"So low," Archer agreed. "She needs to pay."

"Let's not get in trouble," Isla said. "Let's just focus on beating them."

"Or pranking them." Jade still looked ready to attack. "We could do the Sharpie thing with the hearts. I'll help."

Archer's laughter cut across the woods. "That's *exactly* what we'll do."

* * *

The moment Cassandra said goodnight and went to hang out with the other counselors, Archer and Jade crept down the steps and cut through the woods toward Bluebird Cabin. Archer's heart pounded in her chest. They had to time this just right to get back in time before bed check at eleven. If Cassandra came back before then, Lauren was supposed to fake sick and beg to go to the infirmary, before their counselor noticed the pillows stuffed under their sheets.

It was all pretty risky. Archer was just about to call the whole thing off when Jade poked her in the arm, grinning.

"Relax," Jade whispered. "This is going to be great."

"What if we get caught?" Archer asked, ducking to avoid a tree branch. It was hard to see in the dark, and she'd already been scratched on the face more times than she cared to count.

"Cassandra is not going to catch us," Jade scoffed. "And we're not going to get caught at the Bluebirds', either. Their counselor manages all the cabins in the cluster, so there's no chance she'll be in there. We should be fine as long as we're quiet."

Still.

The sticks on the ground seemed to crackle with every careful step. Mosquitoes hummed by Archer's ears, and overhead, bats darted through the trees. Her neck prickled, and Archer froze. Was something watching them? Isla's paranoia about bears kicked in, and her stomach dropped.

You can't quit now. Hang in there.

Bluebird Cabin loomed into sight at the edge of the forest, like some enchanted castle. Cobwebs and dead bugs lined the screen. Now that her eyes had adjusted to the darkness, she could see the eerie outlines of her sister and her friends in their beds. They were fast asleep.

"Boots," Jade mouthed, pointing down. "Too loud."

Archer nodded. Sliding them off, she hid them behind a nearby pine tree. Then she tiptoed to the front door and slid Jade's nail file under the latch. Jade gave her a thumbs-up as the latch lifted.

The slow, measured breathing of the Bluebirds echoed through the room. Before she could lose her nerve, Archer popped the cap off the pink Sharpie and drew a heart on the forehead of the girl closest to her. The girl stirred, and Archer froze.

What if she wakes up?

Archer made eye contact with Jade, whose horrified expression almost sent Archer into a series of panicked giggles. Instead, the girl with the heart on her forehead let out a little sigh and then rolled over.

Once the remaining Bluebirds were equally decorated, Archer climbed the ladder to set the marker next to her snoozing sister.

To her surprise, Makayla was wearing the pink satin sleep mask with the outrageous eyelashes Archer had given her one Christmas. In the moment, Makayla had tossed it aside and declared it "painfully tacky." Now, Archer felt a pang.

I wish things could be different.

One of the Bluebirds coughed in her sleep. Quickly, Archer dropped the pink marker onto Makayla's pillow.

But they're not. So, talk your way out of this one, sis.

* * *

The next morning, Archer couldn't stop giggling on the walk to breakfast. The thought of the Bluebirds waking up, looking in the mirror, and thinking her sister had drawn on their faces with a Sharpie was hilarious. The night before, the Fireflies had laughed at their play-by-play for ten minutes straight.

"I wish we could have been at the window this morning when they woke up," Lauren said, as if reading Archer's mind. "We would have had a front-row seat!"

Everyone giggled except for Jade. She was quiet this morning, with puffy eyes. Archer suspected she had woken up crying.

You'd think if you went to sleep laughing, you wouldn't wake up crying.

That wasn't always the case, though, with Jade. Catching her eye, Archer gave her a small smile. Jade smiled back but then looked away, out at the pine trees.

Yep. She's sad again. I wish I could do more to help her.

The girls walked up the steps and into the front of the mess hall, the scent of bacon thick in the air.

"Has anyone caught up with us?" Lauren stopped in front of the competition board and studied it.

Archer joined her. The Fireflies were still in first place, with 280 points. It was unlikely anyone could have done enough bonus activities to catch them, but not impossible. She gave Lauren a backward high five.

"We'll be at three eighty by this afternoon," Archer said.

"Let's not get overconfident." Isla wrung her hands. "I could pass out today and fall face-first off the stage."

"Then we'll make it up in the relay race." Lauren patted her arm. "Here's the song order for today. Let's see where we're at."

Lauren pulled a piece of paper out of a folder labeled "Information" and skimmed through it. Archer peered at it over her shoulder, noting that the Bluebirds were early in the show. The Fireflies were almost last.

"We're going to crush it," Archer said, whacking Isla on the back.

"If you knock the wind out of me, I won't be able to sing," Isla huffed, then stalked into the mess hall. The other Fireflies burst out laughing and raced after her.

Archer loved the feeling she got from walking across the cafeteria with her friends. They'd scatter to get food, then meet back at their table as quickly as possible, already giggling about some silly thing that had happened. Like the time Isla tried to get orange juice and the machine spit out cranberry juice instead. One of the Butterflies had insisted it was orange juice, no matter how many times the counselors tried to explain there had been a mistake.

"The juice wasn't even orange," Isla kept saying, baffled, and Lauren, Archer, and Jade had screamed with laughter. Silly stuff that no one else would get, unless they'd experienced the story firsthand.

Back home, Archer had witnessed girls acting like this, and it had always bugged her. She'd think, *Do they have to giggle with their friends about everything? Why can't they be more independent?* Now, she knew the answer: Because it was fun to joke that the pan of oatmeal looked like mashed brains or to rate how runny the eggs were each morning on a scale of one to ten. It was fun to have *friends*, something that really bummed her out every time she thought about going back home.

Don't think about it. There's plenty of time left here. Besides, we'll video chat, group text, all of it. I'll still be with them, no matter what.

The Fireflies had just reached the line with the breakfast trays when Isla nearly choked. "The Bluebirds," she whispered.

The Fireflies tensed with anticipation. Out of the corner of her eye, Archer saw her sister strut into the cafeteria. And she heard the fascinated hush that followed her wherever she went.

Archer almost snorted as she stared down at the gray counter, gripping her plastic tray tight. "I'm going to look."

"*Don't,*" Lauren warned, barely moving her lips. "Everyone go get breakfast and meet at the table like always. Or they'll *know* it was us."

The Fireflies split up. Isla and Lauren got in the hot breakfast line, like always, Jade headed for the fruit bar, while Archer made a beeline for the cereal display. She focused on filling up a bowl with Fruity Pebbles, and only then did she glance at the Bluebirds.

They look like walking valentines!

When Archer had gotten herself under control enough to look again, something seemed off. The Bluebirds weren't shooting her sister mean looks or ignoring her altogether. They were giggling with her like always. And…Archer squinted. Her sister had a heart on her forehead too.

What?! That wasn't the plan.

Archer stomped over to the Firefly table. Lauren and Isla were already there. To emphasize her irritation, she slammed her cereal down, sloshing half of it onto the table.

Lauren grabbed a handful of napkins and wiped it up. "I know. It's terrible. Do you think your sister woke up first?"

"Who knows?" Archer grumbled. "It's just my luck."

Jade slid into a chair, setting down a tray with a bowl of cottage cheese, melon, and fresh strawberries. Archer grabbed a strawberry and shoved it into her mouth.

"Take them all," Jade mumbled. "I'm not hungry."

They sat in silence for a moment.

"The worst part..." Lauren drizzled maple syrup over a plate of pancakes and then gave Archer a worried look. "Should I even tell you?"

It was hard to imagine anything could be worse.

"Get it over with."

"It's become a thing," Lauren said. "Some of the younger girls are drawing hearts on *their* foreheads."

Archer's mouth dropped open. "Heinous. Who?"

"The Cherries and the Crabapples," Lauren said before taking a quick bite of bacon.

Isla nodded. "It's kind of cute."

Cute?!

Next to her, Jade put her head in her hands.

"Thank you," Archer mumbled. "At least someone's on my side."

"It's not that." Jade lifted her head, rubbing her nose. In a flat voice, she said, "That's how it used to be at school. The other girls would copy us every time Kiara and I did something new." She stared blankly out at the lake. "I bet everyone misses her. I never really thought of that." Archer didn't have the first clue what to say. There were still moments when she wanted to be mad at Jade for having it so easy, but she also knew how stupid that thought was. Jade didn't have it easy. It didn't matter how pretty she was or that everyone she met wanted to be her friend. Every day was a struggle.

She touched Jade's arm. "You okay?"

Jade reached for her water and downed it in one gulp. "Fine."

Lauren gave her a gentle smile. "Let us know if you're not. We're here for you."

"You know what?" Jade snapped, pushing her chair away from the table. "I'm not going to be happy every second of the day. Sometimes you're just going to have to deal with that."

The other Fireflies sat in silence, watching her go. Just then, one of the Robins ran by, clutching a handful of Sharpies and waving them at her friends.

Archer drained the colorful milk from her cereal bowl. "Well, Isla, I hope you really don't pass out during the singing competition. Because to be honest, it's shaping up to be that kind of day."

Chapter Twenty

The outdoor pavilion at the boys' camp smelled like sweat, cedar, and lake water. Isla would have been disgusted by the smell before camp started, but now she wanted to bottle it like a well-loved perfume. The fact that Jordan would soon be somewhere in this very amphitheater made her heart pound with excitement.

The boys were supposed to sit on the wooden benches, fifteen or so rows back, while the girls sat in the front rows, but the boys hadn't yet arrived. Isla wanted to look over her shoulder to watch for Jordan but didn't dare. She tried to focus on the festive feeling in the air instead of the fact that, before she knew it, she'd be singing onstage. The thought made her stomach clench with nerves.

"You doing okay?" Lauren asked for the fiftieth time, and Isla nodded.

It was obvious Lauren was in a panic about the competition. The idea of letting her down was even worse than the thought of passing out and falling face-first off the stage. She fidgeted, half hoping for a natural disaster. If a lightning storm hit, or even a tornado, the entire thing would get canceled. Unfortunately, the sky gleamed bright blue.

"Don't be nervous." Archer kicked her boots against the dirt floor of the outdoor auditorium. "Focus on what matters: the pig roast afterward."

Isla made a face. "I don't eat pork."

"More for me," Archer said cheerfully.

The counselors had planned a coed celebration down by the beach, complete with pig roast. Everyone was supposed to swim and participate in balloon tosses and potato sack races all day, followed by a big bonfire with fireworks at the end of the night. The whole thing sounded hot, sweaty, and disgusting. The only thing that made the thought bearable was the idea of hiding out somewhere in the shade to spy on Jordan and his friends.

Assuming I'm not being rushed away in an ambulance for passing out and falling face-first off the stage.

Taylor took center stage with one of the counselors from the boys' camp. They both had microphones, and suddenly, music blasted out over the loudspeakers.

"A bright Blueberry Pine and Blueberry Lane welcome," Taylor cried. "Everyone, get on your feet!"

An upbeat version of "The Star-Spangled Banner" started to play, and suddenly, there were a hundred or so boys crowding the stage, singing a rousing rendition of the national anthem. They each held a small flag, and a few of them waved around sparklers.

The girls cheered, jumping up and down while singing along. Isla scanned the crowded stage and almost passed out when she spotted Jordan. He stood over to the side with a group of boys, looking serious and waving a flag.

"Is that him?" Lauren whispered, nodding in his direction.

"Shh!" Isla's entire body went hot with mortification. "Don't look!"

Jordan could not catch her staring at him. That would be the height of humiliation.

The national anthem ended and the boys launched into a joyful rendition of "America the Beautiful." They filed off the stage and into the outdoor auditorium amid applause and cheers, giving shy smiles to the girls. Isla gave a sidelong look at Jordan as he walked by, noting that his hair was now sun streaked and he had an even better tan than she remembered.

"All right, campers," Taylor said, back on the mic. "Shall we get this competition started?"

The audience cheered, and Isla took in a deep breath. It wasn't too late to run screaming for the door. Or maybe it was, because her legs were paralyzed with fear.

Isla watched the other performances in tortured silence. Taylor returned to the stage after each one with an applause meter, and the Fireflies cheered and stomped their feet in support. At least, until the Bluebirds pranced onstage. Their pink Sharpie hearts glowed from their foreheads, and their costumes twinkled in the muted light.

"Oh, they look so stupid," Archer groaned.

The lights flashed on. Makayla gave a huge smile and kicked off the dance routine. The hip shaking and sass was pretty impressive, really. Definitely not something Isla could have done, especially in front of people. Some girl sang for maybe thirty seconds, then took a bow in a frenzied flashing of lights.

The audience roared.

Lauren sat back on the bench with a huff. "This is not good. We can't afford for them to place!"

Isla chewed on her lip, feeling more frightened by the second.

The only other standout performance was the Cardinals, because they were so, so bad. They did some mash-up of a Top 10 hit and the Blueberry Pine camp song, but it made no sense. The boys booed, and the camp counselors stopped everything to lecture them. The Butterflies were on stage when Cassandra beckoned at the Fireflies.

"Come on, girls," she sang, braces flashing. "You're up!"

Isla clutched Lauren's hand as they walked up the rickety steps leading backstage. "I don't think I can do this." Everything felt like it was spinning beneath her.

"You have to!" Lauren's other hand dug into her shoulder. "We need you, Isla. Besides, think of how impressed you-know-who will be."

The Butterflies rushed off the stage in a flurry of giggles, and Taylor held up the applause meter. Cassandra rummaged in a large bin and then handed the Fireflies their prop: a large, silver-sequined sheet that Isla would hide behind. Then Cassandra gave them each high fives.

"Make me proud. You're on in thirty seconds."

The audience cheered for the Butterflies. Suddenly,

Isla imagined stepping out on the stage, and her chest went tight.

No. Not now.

If she had an asthma attack, she wouldn't be able to sing. The fear made her feel faint, and she let go of Lauren's hand and grabbed for a wooden beam attached to the wall. With her other hand, she fumbled in her pocket to make sure she had her inhaler.

"Isla, are you all right?" Lauren asked.

She couldn't answer.

"Fireflies, help," Lauren cried.

The other Fireflies swarmed around Isla. Lauren pulled her hand off the beam and bounced it up and down.

"Zap, zap, zap," she cried, then the rest of the Fireflies joined in.

"Zap, zap, zap!"

The first notes of their music started.

"Go," Cassandra cried.

There was nowhere to run. Lauren pushed her onstage, and the spotlight was so bright, Isla couldn't see any of the faces in the audience. Instead, she noticed a trickle of sweat dripping down Archer's neck, the pink shimmer of Jade's lip gloss, and the flyaway strands of Lauren's bright red hair.

The opening bars faded, and the Fireflies covered Isla with the sparkling sheet. For a split second, she imagined she was back at home, winning competitions with her choir. Taking in a deep breath, she lifted the microphone and forced herself to sing.

The sound of her voice rang out strong, sure, and sweet.

The calm feeling that filled her heart when she sang swept through her like a smile, along with the sense of surprise she always felt that the sound came from her. The pulse and rhythm of the music built, and the Fireflies lowered the sheet to reveal her as the singer.

By then, Isla didn't care. She was lost in the music, the melody soaring out across the water to the wind through the trees, chasing after the clouds in the sky. Before she knew it, the song had hit the crescendo and she let loose the final note.

Stunned silence stretched through the crowd, followed by thunderous applause.

The sudden noise jolted Isla out of her reverie. Embarrassed, she scurried offstage. The other Fireflies rushed after her, jumping up and down as Taylor rated the audience reaction with the applause meter.

"That was incredible," Archer cried, lifting Isla in a hug. "You're amazing!"

Jade gave a serious nod. "You have such a beautiful voice."

"Do you think he liked it?" she whispered.

"Definitely!" Lauren laughed. "And I'm sure he's in love."

The Fireflies giggled hysterically and ran back to their seats. People kept offering Isla congratulations, and she gave little smiles, but ducked her head. She didn't feel right accepting praise for her talent. It wasn't like her Internet business, where she had to work hard to be successful. Singing was a gift, like Archer's ability to be funny.

Or Jordan's ability to be gorgeous.

Had he recognized her? The thought made her cheeks flush bright red.

There were four other acts. Isla focused on taking deep breaths to calm down, because her heart was still racing. Finally, the event ended and Taylor took to the stage to announce the winners.

"Third place goes to the Strawberries," she cried.

The Fireflies applauded loud and long for the group of younger girls.

Isla gripped the rough edge of the bench. What if they didn't place at all?

I'll smile and be gracious, she decided. *That's all I can do.*

The smell of cinnamon was suddenly strong, and she turned to see Archer shoving a bunch of gum into her mouth. Lauren noticed, too, and frowned. Reaching over, she counted the wrappers.

"Three pieces?" Lauren demanded. "Isn't that a little excessive?"

"I'm nervous," Archer said, chomping away.

"Second place goes to..." Taylor smiled at the audience. "The Bluebirds."

"Ugh." Archer kicked the floor with her boots.

"Oh no." Lauren looked super-depressed. "That is not good for us."

The Bluebirds ran to the stage, and Jade shook her head. "Yeah, but we saw that one coming."

Lauren bit her nails.

"Finally, first place goes to..." Taylor put her fist into the air. "Once again, the Fireflies!"

There was a loud roar in Isla's ears, and for a split second, the amphitheater seemed to go quiet, even though everyone was clapping. Isla flushed hot and then cold and felt stuck to the bench. Then Lauren grabbed her hands.

"Come on," she cried, pulling Isla to her feet. "You did it!"

"We did it," Isla said, and her friends cheered.

The Fireflies raced up the wooden steps to enthusiastic applause. Isla glanced out at the audience, and her heart nearly stopped. Jordan was looking right at her, a goofy smile on his face. Of course Lauren noticed.

"Let's wait outside to talk to him," she whispered. "Okay?"

"Zap, zap," Archer cried, waving their trophy.

The Fireflies giggled, and Isla nodded, grinning from ear to ear.

* * *

They waited for Jordan next to the exit of the amphitheater. Isla's silk shirt was damp with sweat, and the breeze from the lake felt cool against her skin. Lauren practically bounced up and down in anticipation, while Jade and Archer headed to the beach.

A steady stream of campers passed by and Isla fidgeted. The anxiety was really starting to get to her.

"I don't want to do this," she finally said, swatting away a mosquito. "We need to have time to apply sunscreen and get water before the activities start. Let's go."

"No way." Lauren stepped in front of her. "This is your

one chance to bump into him without making it obvious. Stop looking so stressed out. Pretend like we're just standing here, having a conversation."

The stream of campers trickled down to none. The only sign of life was a bumblebee that seemed determined to dive-bomb Isla as many times as possible.

Lauren looked puzzled. "Did we miss him?"

Maybe. Even though the campers had been instructed to leave through this exit, there was another that led to the beach. Maybe Jordan and his friends had decided to break the rules.

Disappointed, Isla shrugged. "It doesn't matter. Let's go."

She was just about to turn away when Jordan and his friends raced out. They ran right past, and she thought he hadn't seen her, until he stopped suddenly and looked back over his shoulder. Their eyes met and Isla's legs nearly gave out beneath her.

What am I doing? It's so obvious I like him.

Of course, the bee picked that moment to buzz by. Isla involuntarily shrieked and swatted at it, which was super-embarrassing.

Lauren leaned in. "Laugh," she instructed. "Like I'm saying something funny."

Isla forced a laugh, feeling ridiculous. Jordan tapped one of his friends on the back, pointing toward them. Then he and the group of boys headed back their way.

Isla felt incredibly stupid—until Jordan looked right at her (!) and said, "You sound like Adele."

"No, I don't," she said, blushing.

He grinned. "You gonna sneak back onstage or are you coming to the beach? They're roasting a pig."

The idea of a pig on a spit was less revolting when the words came from Jordan's lips.

"We're headed to the beach." She gave an eager nod. "We were just…"

"Waiting for the rest of the girls in our cabin, but I bet we missed them," Lauren said quickly. "Let's go."

To Isla's horror, Lauren rushed forward and started talking to Jordan's friends, leaving her to walk alone with him. He still smelled like grape Jolly Ranchers and fresh cotton. She pinched the inside of her wrist, wondering if she'd passed out onstage and was dreaming this entire encounter.

For a moment, the birds in the trees made the only sound. Then Jordan spoke. "How did you do that? Sing like that?"

Isla hesitated. "I don't know." Normally, she would have left it at that, but he was looking at her the way people looked at her brothers: like she was something great. "I've always been able to sing. However, I prefer not to sing in front of other people. I become exceptionally nervous."

"You could've fooled me."

She sneaked a peek at him. He had a small scar by his ear, an imperfection that made him even more perfect.

"It's one of those things where I kind of forget about everything. Even though I'm nervous at first, it's like something takes over. This sense of calm."

He gave an eager nod. "It's like that when I play basketball.

I don't hear the crowd or think about anything; only the swish the ball makes through the net. It's one of the few things I don't feel pressured at, because I know I'm really good at it."

Isla was surprised he felt pressured too. "My parents want me to be so good at everything," she blurted out. "They want me to be a surgeon."

"Mine too!" He held up his hands, laughing. "My hands are enormous. The patients would run screaming."

Isla smiled. His hands were, in fact, the size of bear claws.

The sidewalk turned into steps that led to the beach. Once they hit the sand, one of Jordan's friends turned back and called, "Is Adele teaching you how to sing?"

Jordan laughed again. "I gotta go hang out with those losers. Could I sit next to you at the bonfire?"

The sand seemed to shift under her feet. She squeaked out, "Please do."

"Cool." Jordan jogged up to his friends. They took off, wrestling and flipping one another over the others' backs. He glanced back at her once and grinned.

Lauren rushed over and squeezed her arm. "Tell me everything."

"He asked to sit with me at the bonfire," she managed to say.

Lauren cheered. "He loooooooves you."

Did that just happen? Did I really just talk to Jordan?

"I l-love camp," Isla stammered.

Lauren giggled, and the two rushed to meet the rest of the Fireflies. Suddenly, the world seemed full of possibility.

Chapter Twenty-One

Lauren climbed the steps of the bus waiting in the parking lot. The fireworks were over; the Fireflies were exhausted; and Isla stood to the side, saying a shy good night to Jordan. Plus, with their win, the Fireflies now had 380 points in the Faces of Blueberry Pine competition! The day could not have been more perfect.

The bus smelled like exhaust and hair spray, and the seats were packed with fellow campers. Jade and Archer grabbed the first open seat. Lauren slid in behind them, saving the seat next to her for Isla. The Bluebirds started the bird chant, and along with everyone on the bus, Lauren turned to watch.

> Birds of a feather
> We all flock together
> Rain or shine
> We'll be fine
> We'll flap our wings
> Then we'll sing
> Tra-la-li-la-la

Tra-la-li-la-la

O the freedom

We can fly

Tra-la-li-la-la

On the final part, the bird cabins flapped their wings so hard it was a wonder the bus didn't lift up into the sky. Then they all giggled.

From the front of the bus, there was an audible sigh. "I can't wait until we're old enough to do that."

Lauren sat back against the seat.

What would it be like to come back to camp every single year? To be with the Fireflies, again and again?

In a word, it would be amazing. Everything in her life would be easier, knowing she had friends like this. Ever since the night swim, tiny thoughts like that had been nagging at her, and they were progressively more daring.

Make it last.

You don't have to say goodbye.

Maybe you could find a way to come back.

It was that thought that really struck her. Could she really find a way to come to camp again next year?

Aren't you fancy, one of the meanest foster mothers used to say, whenever Lauren had big ideas. *Always wanting more. Get ready to be disappointed, because girls like you aren't nothing special at all.*

The words hurt, but Lauren refused to believe them. Every time she set a goal and worked hard to reach it, good things happened. Like winning the scholarship to come to camp in the first place. Maybe she could win another scholarship to come back? No, the rules stated it was impossible to receive the award twice. That option was out, so what could she do?

Get creative, her English teacher always said. *If the answer isn't right in front of you, start searching for it.*

There had to be a solution. It was just a matter of finding it.

Lauren's thoughts returned to the present when Isla walked down the aisle of the bus, her pale face flushed with excitement. She slid in next to Lauren and folded her hands in her lap. Archer and Jade hung over the back of the seat, waiting for her to speak.

"Well?" Archer finally demanded.

Isla cleared her throat, obviously enjoying the drama.

"Tell us," Jade insisted. "Come on."

The bus lurched out of the camp parking lot, and Isla gave them a big smile. Then she launched into a detailed description of her night with Jordan.

"He even held my hand during the grand finale of the fireworks," she said, blushing.

Lauren held her breath. "Did he kiss you? Outside the bus?"

"Of course not." Isla covered her face with her hands. She splayed her fingers and grinned. "But he's going to call me during Indoor Rec."

The other Fireflies cheered.

Archer started their secret handshake.

"Zap, zap, zzzzzap," they cried.

For once, Isla shouted louder than anyone.

Lauren leaned against the window, the wind warm on her cheeks.

The Fireflies are meant to be friends forever.

She just had to figure out how to make it happen.

* * *

The feeling stuck with her through the following week. Finally, during Indoor Rec, Lauren decided to ask to help out in the kitchen for a few hours. Baking soothed her, and she hoped it would quiet the confusion in her heart. No matter how many times she tried to focus on the here and now, she couldn't shake the disbelief that she had already been at camp for four weeks and in no time at all, the Fireflies would be a distant memory.

When Lauren walked into the kitchen, it was steaming hot. Chef was hard at work, her round cheeks flushed.

"Well, aren't you a glutton for punishment," Chef said when Lauren asked to help. There were dirty dishes stacked everywhere, loaves of bread rising on the oven, and several bags of onions next to a cutting board. "Dishes or chopping onions. You pick."

"Chopping." Cheerfully, Lauren grabbed a knife. "I've already cried in this kitchen once. Might as well do it again."

Chef chuckled. They worked in companionable silence, falling into the steadying rhythm of the knives against the cutting board. Once the space was so full they couldn't cut any more, Chef dumped the contents into a large bowl and they began chopping once again.

"What's your story, missy?" Chef said after ten minutes. "There's more to you than meets the eye."

Lauren hesitated. From the beginning, Lauren had suspected Chef could see right through her.

"Do you really want to know?" she asked.

Chef wiped her face with her apron. "If you want to tell me." Her voice was gentle. "I get the impression you've got something you want to hide."

Lauren chewed on her lip. Lying was getting old. So, as they diced the next round of onions, she told Chef the truth.

"It's been hard," she admitted. "I knew camp would be incredible, but I thought it would be easy to say goodbye."

Chef added the last of the onions to the bowl. Then, she pulled out a five-pound bag of carrots, fresh cutting boards, and two peelers. "That's the thing about the good life. Once you taste it, it's hard to go back to plain potatoes."

Lauren grabbed a peeler to help. "It's the Fireflies, really. I'll never get to see them again, which is pretty typical for me. My parents died when I was three and I've never lived with a family for longer than a year. I'm used to saying goodbye. It's just that saying goodbye to these girls seems so hard."

Chef thought for a moment. "Can't you win another scholarship?"

"No," Lauren said. "It's in the rules."

Chef's face brightened. "Ask to work here!"

Lauren's heart skipped a beat. "They do that?"

"Not that I've seen, but it never hurts to ask." Chef swiped the peels into the garbage. "I could use the help. You know your way around a kitchen."

Lauren jumped up and down. "Thank you, thank you, thank you!"

"Look into it, but don't get too excited yet," Chef warned. "It's just an idea."

Lauren beamed. "It's brilliant."

Grabbing the carrots, she peeled in earnest.

I could work here next year. And every year. It doesn't have to be over, and I could be the one singing about freedom and flapping my wings.

Chef pointed at the clock. "It's getting about time for you to head on."

It was nearly three o'clock, time for Lauren's elective. This week, she was on a team for beach volleyball. It was a blast.

"Thank you." She beamed at Chef. "You don't know how much this means to me."

Lauren banged the kitchen door shut with glee. Then she flew through the forest to the beach, feeling like she might truly have wings.

Chapter Twenty-Two

Jade's legs were tangled in a rope underwater. She couldn't get away, no matter how hard she kicked.

No one noticed, either, because Makayla was lounging on a raft with Colin. She wore a polka-dotted suit and was sharing a picnic with him. Neither of them seemed to mind that Jade was trapped below, gasping for air.

A hand gripped her shoulder.

"Jade."

Blinking, she turned to the side.

Isla peered at her. "You were having a nightmare."

Jade brushed away tears. The springs of the bed overhead came into focus. Her sheets were damp with sweat. Outside the window, the trees were a dark outline against the early morning sky.

"Sorry I woke you up," Jade mumbled.

"It's okay." Isla pressed skinny arms against her silk nightgown. "I'm a light sleeper." She held out a bottle of water. "Drink this. If you want it."

"Thanks." Jade took the water and held it tight. "I think I'm going to get up." The thought of another nightmare was terrifying.

"Do you mind if I sleep a little while longer?" Isla asked. "It's only six thirty."

Jade shook her head. "Thanks for checking on me."

The springs on Isla's bed creaked from across the room, and Jade slid in her earbuds. She blasted hip-hop, trying to drown out the images in her head. It didn't work. The panic of the dream still clutched at her heart.

Climbing out of bed, she surveyed the cabin.

Lauren was out on her walk and Cassandra's cot was made. Isla and Archer were fast asleep. The cabin smelled of bonfire smoke from last night's campfire.

Pushing open the screen door, she settled into the rocking chair on the front porch. It had been a strange few weeks, making new friends and, for the first time in ages, having fun. The Fireflies made her laugh the way Kiara had made her laugh. Even more, they were there for her, like when Isla woke her from the nightmare. Without the Fireflies, she would be forced to face her fear and heartache alone. It was hard to believe how much these girls had come to mean to her in such a short period of time.

"Good morning," chirped a voice, interrupting her thoughts.

Jade jumped. "Oh, hey."

Cassandra climbed the porch steps, already chewing a

huge piece of gum. "It's Archer's birthday tomorrow. Here's a card from the counselors. Do you guys have something special planned?"

"Oh." Jade took the envelope. "No, she didn't tell us."

Archer's birthday was coming up?

Jade couldn't believe she hadn't said a word about it.

"Hmm..." Cassandra popped a bubble. "She might be shy about it. Some people are."

"Shy or not, we have to do something," Jade said, and their counselor nodded.

"Let me know what I can do to help. I wanted to swing this by, but for now, I've got to head out and help update the leaderboards for the contest."

"How are we doing?" Jade asked. "We just did a bunch of the bonus points."

"In all your spare time?" Cassandra teased.

Camp was definitely busy. This week, the Insects had learned to fly-fish, taken a Red Cross course on CPR, and mastered a hip-hop routine in dance class. Still, the Fireflies had managed to complete three bonus activities for the competition: they'd made a model of their cabin only using items from nature, recited a funny jingle about Blueberry Pine onstage at lunch, and planted a tree in the arbor.

"The Fireflies are crushing it," Cassandra said. "Keep it up."

Lauren climbed the front steps as Cassandra left.

"What are you doing up?" Lauren asked. She clutched a bag, most likely filled with cinnamon donuts.

Sure enough, she offered her one. Jade shook her head and held out the card.

"It's Archer's birthday tomorrow."

"Did you know?" Lauren looked miffed.

"No clue. She might not want us to know."

Lauren's face fell. "We can't *not* celebrate her birthday."

Jade stared out at the forest. Then an idea struck her and she smiled. "I know exactly what we're going to do."

Chapter Twenty-Three

Uggh. Talk about a sucky birthday.

In truth, Archer's birthdays had sucked for a few years. She never celebrated anymore. Wanda, her one and only friend back home, thought birthdays were stupid: the cake, the presents, but mainly, the enthusiasm.

"It's not like you did anything special to be born," Wanda liked to snarl. "Why are we supposed to get excited?"

It felt weird to not tell the Fireflies, but what if they felt the same? That would be embarrassing. So, she kept the news that she'd turned twelve to herself.

During Indoor Rec, the Fireflies scattered. Even Jade. Feeling depressed, Archer headed to the art building on her own.

The young campers were in another painting class. She gave them a weak smile as she passed.

I hope you guys never have a sucky birthday.

In the back of the room, she went to pull her project out of the slot and stopped. It was gone. Dread settled in the pit of her stomach.

Yes, it was possible the counselors had cleaned out the bins. But the painting next to hers, some terrible version of the lake that had irritated her all week, still sat there wallowing in its talentless glory.

Archer stomped out to the front porch. Mallory, her least favorite counselor, sat in the sun, reading a book.

"Someone stole my painting," Archer growled.

Mallory squinted. "What do you mean?"

"I can't find my painting," she repeated, feeling dumb.

Mallory sighed and dog-eared her book. "Sometimes they get filed in the wrong slot." She got to her feet and headed inside.

Archer followed. Normally, the smell of the chalky pastels inspired her. Now, they made her feel sick.

Mallory flipped through the files in the back. "Isn't this it?" She held it up. The look on her face was pure distaste, like she could only expect someone with Kool-Aid hair to paint something so hideous.

Because Archer's painting was now, indeed, hideous.

Someone—take a wild guess who—had covered it in graffiti. The sunset now looked apocalyptic and had "pathetic" blazed across it. The sign above Firefly Cabin read "losers." And all the beautiful, sparkling fireflies in the woods were blacked out.

"This is so angry," Mallory tsked. "Is everything all right?"

What can I say? It would be impossible to prove I didn't write all that.

"I'm great," Archer said. "But thanks so much for your feedback."

Mallory gave her a look before returning to the porch.

Archer sat in silence, staring at the destruction.

What am I supposed to do with this?

Fix it, she imagined Jade saying. *Just paint over the words.*

Where could she put it, though, where it would be safe? She couldn't trudge back to Firefly Cabin with it every afternoon. It would get ruined.

Like it wasn't already.

My sister is such a jerk.

Archer dumped it in the trash and stomped out the front door. She passed Mallory in an angry blur and rushed toward the Lodge, wishing she could trash Bluebird Cabin instead.

Once there, she dodged past the other campers and their crafts. She yanked on the storage room doors until one opened, cued up Paolo, and fired off a message to her sister.

It's time we met.

* * *

"Archer! There you are," Jade called. "I've been looking all over for you." She bounced onto the couch in the television area, jostling Archer out of a half nap.

Squinting, Archer sat up. The other campers were watching the original *Parent Trap*. Leave it to a movie to show two sisters being the best of friends; reality was a completely different story.

"Hey." Jade tried to hand her a bottle of water, which she pushed away. "Get up. You're supposed to come with me."

Archer pulled her knees to her chest. "Forget it. I'm sleeping."

With an hour left for Indoor Rec, it made no sense for Jade to try and ruin her nap. Especially since Jade was so touchy about napping herself.

"Privacy, please," Archer groaned, because she could still feel Jade's breath on her neck.

"Sorry, you've got to get up." Jade's pretty face was troubled. "Look, I didn't want to say it, but you're in huge trouble. You have a bathroom violation. I was told to go find you."

A *bathroom* violation? Archer had never even heard of such a thing, and now she had one? This was the worst birthday in the history of birthdays.

"I can't believe this," she grumbled, but got to her feet.

It wouldn't be smart to risk a scene. If the counselors had to come and get her, word would get out. The second her sister learned she had a bathroom violation, she'd never hear the end of it.

"We're supposed to go to the kitchen." Jade grimaced. "I think you have to do dishes or something."

Archer complained under her breath the entire way across the main lawn. Jade led her around the back and knocked on the kitchen door.

Like a jail warden, she called, "I've got Archer."

Seriously? Did she have to sound so happy about it?

"Send her in," Cassandra called back.

Archer stomped in. The afternoon light stretched across

the kitchen in long rays. The room smelled delicious, like cinnamon and vanilla, but that did little to quell the rage inside of her. Looking around, she didn't see Cassandra anywhere. Then suddenly, someone yelled, "Surprise!"

Lauren, Isla, Cassandra, and Chef jumped up from behind the gigantic counter. Lauren held up a cake with frosting flowers and twelve sparkling, silver candles. Jade rushed behind the counter with them, and they all began to sing "Happy Birthday."

Archer's mouth dropped open. "Oh my gosh. What...?" Her voice trailed off as she realized the blue and purple flowers on the cake were the same color as her hair. "Wow," she breathed, once they were finished singing. She covered her face with her hands. "This is epic, you guys." Then she erupted into giggles and pointed at Jade. "You said I had a *bathroom violation!*"

The other Fireflies hooted and hollered. Archer took a step forward and looked at the cake, uncertain what to do next.

Lauren sang, "Make a wish."

Of course. It had been so long since she'd celebrated a birthday, she forgot all about that part. Closing her eyes, she wished to be friends with the Fireflies for the rest of her life.

Jade applauded as the candles flickered out. "Your sister's face will be covered in warts by dinner."

Everyone laughed, even Chef. She sliced up pieces of cake for everyone, adding generous helpings of vanilla ice cream. The cake was cinnamon spice with cream cheese icing, something her mother baked for her every year.

"How did you guys know about this?" Archer demanded,

the second she took a bite. In spite of all their heart-to-hearts, she couldn't remember ever telling them her favorite type of cake.

"Cassandra called your mom," Jade said, dipping her fork in the cream cheese. "To find out if you had any traditions."

Archer couldn't believe anyone had gone to this much trouble for her. Digging into her cake, she tried to think of a hundred different ways to say thank you, but every time she tried, she got choked up. Instead, she focused on licking the ice cream off her plate and laughing at Chef's stories of Isla's attempts at cracking an egg without touching the yolk.

"We have presents." Lauren threw away her paper plate and slid forward a bunch of wrapped packages.

The girls had used anything and everything as wrapping paper, from tinfoil to the construction paper they used for crafts during Indoor Rec. It was the most beautiful collection of presents Archer had ever seen. Eagerly, she ripped into them.

Lauren gave her a necklace made out of wire that spelled out "Queen Firefly," Isla gave her a headband embroidered with skulls but no monogram, and Jade's present was the painting she'd been working on: the art room with two blank easels. Cassandra gave her a six-pack of Mountain Dew, and Chef let her have the rest of the cake, wrapped up in tinfoil.

"This birthday rocks," she kept saying, embarrassed by all the attention.

When Chef and Cassandra started talking about camp stuff, she pulled her friends aside. "I want you guys to know how much this means to me. Birthdays have been rotten for a while. You guys made it fun again. You're incredible."

Lauren shook her head. "Archer, you're incredible," she insisted. "I can't imagine being a Firefly without you."

The spice from the cake warmed her tongue as the girls walked back to the cabin. The girls carried the Mountain Dew and leftover cake, while Archer wore her necklace and headband, and carried the painting tucked under one arm. It was the best birthday she'd had in ages, and her heart sang with the knowledge that it was all thanks to her friends.

Chapter Twenty-Four

Isla couldn't remember a time she had been so happy.

Ever since the bonfire, Jordan had called every single day. She loved his sense of humor, the way he teased her about everything, and the fact that their half-hour phone call felt like mere seconds.

She was so excited to see him again at the next competition: a scavenger hunt that would take place at both camps!

The morning of the scavenger hunt, Isla could hardly sit still at breakfast.

I can't wait to see him again. Face-to-face.

Isla planned to surprise him. Not because she was big on surprises, really, but because she didn't feel bold enough to say, "Hey, Jordan. Do you want to set a time to meet during the scavenger hunt?" When she admitted as much to the other Fireflies, they couldn't believe that she wasn't going to say anything.

"Hold up." Archer took a bite of Fruity Pebbles and waved her spoon. "You talk to this guy every day, but you didn't tell him you're going to be within mere feet of him?"

The girls were at breakfast. Isla could barely choke down

a piece of dry toast, but Archer had already polished off two bowls of cereal.

"I didn't want to make plans with him because I'll be competing." Isla squeezed her hands. "There won't be time."

Lauren, Jade, and Archer exchanged glances.

"Well." Lauren patted her hand. "We'll see what we can work out."

Jade grinned. "Get you guys a little private time."

Even though that was Isla's plan, she didn't want to say it out loud. She grabbed her tray, blushing furiously. "Let's stop talking about it, okay?" She stomped away from the table, heart racing a mile a minute. Archer made kissing noises behind her.

Kissing Jordan?

Her palms went damp at the thought.

* * *

The Fireflies weren't nearly as cheerful when the counselors passed out the task list.

Lauren chewed her lip. "This is intense."

It was more complicated than the brain-building activities Isla's parents gave her. There were thirty assignments under three different categories—Object Retrieval, Puzzle It Out, and Blast from the Past. Plus, the difficulty level was based on age.

"It might be harder to beat the younger girls," Isla mused, looking at the list. "Depending on how much of an advantage they were given. That seems unfair."

Lauren looked worried. The Fireflies had placed first twice now, but anyone could pull ahead.

"It'll be okay," Jade said. "I'm pretty good at scavenger hunts. Kiara and I..." She stopped talking suddenly, and Isla touched her arm. Jade let out a breath. "Kiara and I coordinated a huge scavenger hunt at the end of the summer for our friends. We spent most of August setting it up and...I don't know. It made going back to school feel like a celebration."

"That sounds really fun." Archer stretched, showcasing a new drawing on her upper arm. The planets and stars looked cool, but Isla couldn't help but think it had to be giving her some form of ink poisoning. "Of course, I would have solved your clues in a second."

"No chance." Jade took a drink out of her water bottle. "You would have quaked with terror at the stuff we came up with."

"I'm quaking with terror at this." Lauren smoothed the list, which was already damp from the humidity. "Let's plan it out."

Jade and Archer crowded around as Lauren doled out the tasks. Isla hung back, squeezing her hands. Lauren seemed pretty nervous about getting it all done, and Isla hoped she still planned to send Isla to the boys' camp.

"Blueberry Lane has fifteen questions," Lauren said as if reading her mind. "You'll need help."

Jade raised her hand. "Isla and I can partner up."

Good. Jade wouldn't tease her too much about Jordan.

"Okay." Lauren gave a vigorous nod. "There are no rules, other than no Internet. So, let's do it. Zap!"

The Fireflies brought it in for the secret handshake. Then Lauren hopped on a bicycle, racing across the wooden pathways. Archer stomped toward the lake like she was about to take someone prisoner. Isla and Jade headed to the parking lot, where a large van waited to shuttle teams back and forth.

"Scavenger hunt?" the driver asked, and they nodded.

Isla's heart pounded as she climbed the steps.

I'm minutes away! Jordan going to be so surprised to see me.

"Are you nervous?" Jade asked as they settled in.

"Yes." Isla pushed her bangs out of her eyes. "I can't wait to see him, though."

Jade propped her knees against the seat in front of them. "You'll be fine. Once he figures out girls are descending on his turf, he'll keep an eye out for you."

Oh, I hope she's right.

It was one thing to talk to him on the phone. To see him again in person?

The thought was too thrilling for words.

* * *

Isla practically pressed her nose against the window when they pulled into Blueberry Lane. There were groups of boys walking across the main area, but no Jordan. He had told her he liked to eat half a grapefruit and three bowls of cereal every morning for breakfast, so maybe he was busy doing that.

"Pickup is every half hour," the driver said as the girls filed out. "Last pickup is eleven. Don't miss the van. You wouldn't want to stay at the boys' camp."

Jade gave Isla a sidelong look. "Wanna bet?" she murmured, and Isla giggled.

"All right." Jade stood to the side of the parking lot and held up the list. "Let's crush this or Lauren will disown us."

Isla nodded. They were supposed to do a bunch of silly things like take a picture of the boys' cafeteria with an instax mini camera, collect a signature from a camper in each age category, and even get one of the boys to give them a sock from their uniform. (Gross.)

"We'll need to divide and conquer." Jade clicked her tongue against the roof of her mouth. "I'll take the picture and do the history stuff. You can do this puzzle with the main sign, get signatures from the boys, and collect the things we need. Jordan would definitely give you a sock."

Isla broke into hysterical giggles. "Yuck!"

Jade smiled. "Let's meet back at the flagpole every hour to check in. Good luck. Go get him."

Isla felt the first twinge of panic as Jade took off, studying her paper as she went. Would it seem totally weird to Jordan that Isla was here, as if she were following him around? Her brothers complained about that with girls all the time.

But I have a real reason to be here.

Plenty of her fellow campers were on the camp's grounds and had already started approaching the boys. It wouldn't seem strange to be one of them, right? It was all so confusing.

Focus on the scavenger hunt. Then worry about Jordan.

Isla looked down at her tasks. The first read "Solve the mystery of the welcome sign. What does the secret message say?" and listed a series of numbers and letters, along with a space for her to fill in the blanks and unscramble a word.

The main sign was right next to the parking lot. Isla joined the cluster of girls already hovering around it. She tried not to listen as the other girls puzzled it out, because the different ages had different questions, and besides, that would be dishonest. Instead, she studied the sign, which read BLUEBERRY LANE, followed by a brief history of the camp.

She had to find the fifth letter in the first row of the camp's history, the twenty-seventh letter in the third row, and so on. It took a few minutes, but the right number of letters finally filled the blank spaces. The only remaining task was to unscramble them.

AFRCEMPI

Finally, she saw it. "Campfire." She covered the paper with her hand. "Good. Only seven tasks left to go."

Then I'll go find him, no matter what.

The next task proved simple, as she quickly found a pen branded with Blueberry Lane. The questions became more challenging when she had to gather objects or information from the boy campers, because they were all in the middle of their daily activities.

Isla had to wait by the ropes obstacle course, the swim area, and the soccer field. It took forever to get the next three questions on her list completed, but she finally pulled it off. Before she knew it, it was time to meet Jade, and she rushed across the camp's grounds.

The boys must have just ended their first round of activities because the pathway was suddenly packed. Isla spotted one of Jordan's friends, the blond boy with the spiked hair, and her heart nearly stopped. Jordan's friends traveled in a pack, so he was here, somewhere, in the chaos.

I'm going to see him. I'm finally going to see him. I'm…

The thought froze, along with her heart. Jordan stood beneath the overhang of the staircase of the performance pavilion. The very place where she and Lauren had waited for him. And he was *hugging* another girl.

How could this happen? Isla had talked to him on the phone eleven times. Eleven!

She'd told him things that she had never told anyone else. Like the time her mother had given her money to give to the doorman and she'd used it to buy a hot cocoa instead. And that her biggest fear was that her business would fail and she wouldn't be able to pay her parents back for the supplies she'd bought to start it.

She'd shared because she'd trusted him. Now, she couldn't believe her eyes.

The girl took a step back. Sally Stephens. She was older than Isla, a Cardinal, and had a loud laugh. Isla had always liked her…until this very moment.

How humiliating. What could she do? What should she say?

Jade. I need to find Jade.

Jordan turned and saw her. He said something to Sally, then jogged over.

"What are you doing here?" he said, smiling.

"Why were you hugging her?" Isla squawked.

"Sally?" Jordan looked surprised. "We're friends from back home. She was upset."

Isla squinted at him in the sun. Was that true? It was hard to know what to believe anymore.

Sally walked past. The flounce in her step did not give any indication she had ever been upset. "I'll call you."

"She'll *call* you?" Isla whispered, outraged.

What would Archer do? What would she say?

Isla took in a shaky breath. "You suck," she said, and rushed away.

The tears were blinding and the trees seemed to blur by. Her skin was hot with humiliation or sunburn; it was hard to tell which. Had she really been so caught up in Jordan that she'd forgotten sunscreen? She needed to get out of there.

"Isla, wait," Jordan called.

Isla yanked on her hat and sunglasses. He would *not* see her cry. The parking lot was steps away, and Jade waited by the flagpole. Isla walked right past her, straight for the van.

"Hey," Jade called, waving.

Isla took the steps two at a time. That wasn't safe, but she was too upset to care. Moments later, Jade joined her.

"Hey." Jade slid her sunglasses back on her head. "What happened?"

Isla didn't answer. Instead, she leaned forward, grabbed Jade, and burst into tears.

Chapter Twenty-Five

Lauren sat in the tiny lobby of the administration building, twisting her hands together. She'd set up a meeting with Carol Kennedy, the director of Outreach Services, to discuss the possibility of working in the kitchen next year. The meeting was during Indoor Rec, which was hardly good timing.

Isla was a mess after what had happened with Jordan. She needed all the Fireflies by her side. Lauren hated that she couldn't be there, but if she succeeded at this meeting, she could be there for years to come. If she didn't…well, that was too painful to consider.

Not to mention the pressure the Fireflies were now under in the Faces of Blueberry Pine competition. They didn't even place in the scavenger hunt because they had seven wrong answers.

Seven.

Isla had left the boys' camp after the thing with Jordan, and Jade hadn't had the time to finish without her—she had four blanks. Then the Fireflies missed three other answers.

Lauren wasn't mad at Isla for leaving Blueberry Lane. But their lead was now at risk. They only had 440 points, and the Bluebirds were now at four hundred, and Lauren seemed to be the only Firefly upset about it.

Am I the only one taking the contest seriously?

"Lauren?" A woman with a stern expression and bobbed gray hair walked into the waiting room. "I'm Carol Kennedy. It's nice to meet you."

"Hi!" Lauren leaped to her feet and shook the director's hand. "Thank you so much for awarding me the scholarship. I absolutely love it here."

"Wonderful." The woman shook her hand in return and led her down the hallway. The administration building was small and rustic, like most buildings at Blueberry Pine, with wooden walls and hardwood floors. "The administration was intrigued by your request. We're looking forward to discussing it with you further."

Lauren's heart pounded with excitement.

Mrs. Kennedy led her into a small meeting room that smelled like cologne, where two women and an older man were seated. They greeted her with friendly smiles.

"We appreciated your proposal," the man said, once introductions had been made. "Why don't you tell us more about what you're picturing?"

Lauren wiped her hands on her trousers. "Well, the girls in my cabin have become like my family." The adults nodded. "I've been trying to figure out how to come back. I thought that, next year, I could volunteer in the kitchen for two hours each day, helping Chef prep the meals, in exchange for attending camp. It would help me develop skills in cooking, which is a personal passion, as well as afford me the opportunity to continue my time at Blueberry Pine."

The adults looked impressed. Good. Chef had helped Lauren with the wording on that part.

"Wouldn't you miss having that time with your camp mates?" one of the women asked, adjusting her spectacles. "You say that you love the relationships you have with the girls in your cabin. How can you maintain that if you're volunteering in the kitchen?"

"My friends and I are apart for many of our electives," she said. "It's no different."

One of the women shook her head. "But aren't you concerned that it might wear you out? How can you enjoy camp if you're tired?"

Lauren started to feel nervous. Were they looking for reasons to say no?

"I have a lot of energy. Two hours of work is nothing to me, really."

"There's also a confidentiality issue," Mrs. Kennedy pointed out. "We don't reveal scholarship winners to avoid an economic divide. Yet the other girls might notice if you're helping in the kitchen."

Lauren pressed her hands against the table. "I guess that's a small price to pay if it means I get to see my friends again."

The man nodded. "Well said, Lauren."

She leaned back and crossed her fingers as tightly as she could under the table. "Does that mean I can do it?"

Mrs. Kennedy got to her feet. "There is still a lot to discuss. You certainly have given us food for thought. We'll let you know when we come to a decision or if we have further questions. Thank you for taking the time to meet with us."

Lauren's mouth felt dry as she left the building. Outside, she leaned against the side wall and stared up at the sky.

Please. Please let them say yes.

Chapter Twenty-Six

Archer slid down to a sitting position in a broom closet and pulled out her phone. A message was waiting, and she paused. What if Makayla didn't want to meet Paolo? Letting out a breath, she clicked on it.

I would love to meet you. How, though? When? I can't wait to hold you in my arms.

Archer leaped to her feet and did a victory dance.

Revenge! It's finally happening. But when?

The counselors were having this big group bonfire on the second to last week of camp. Everyone was talking about it, even though it was supposed to be a secret. That would be the perfect time to sneak out without getting caught. No one would try to stop her but Jade.

Archer's black nail polish flew over the keys: I have a modeling gig booked in Detroit—not this Monday, but next. I'll come up to camp. Meet the Bluebirds. Show everyone what true love looks like.

Archer stopped typing. Thanks to Jade, she sometimes

worried that pranking her sister really *was* heinous. But the reasons that Makayla deserved it flashed through her mind: Makayla spreading rumors, destroying her painting, treating her like the scum of the Earth.

Enough is enough.

Actions had consequences. It was time for Makayla to learn that.

Send it.

The message pinged through and she felt light-headed. Then Makayla's sneering face flashed through her mind.

No mercy.

There was a noise outside the door, and Archer jumped. Feeling restless, she slipped out of the broom closet and jogged to the Lodge to get her cabin's mail.

Isla, Jade, and Lauren had letters, which she tucked into her back pocket. As she headed toward the main room, a squealing group of ten-year-olds practically ran her over. The mail scattered across the floor.

"Animals!" Archer yelled at them. "Have some respect for your elders."

The girls ignored her and raced down the hall.

Irritated, Archer stomped around, picking up the mail. Lauren's letter was hanging out of its envelope, and the letter-head caught her eye: "Shady Acres Home for Girls."

Huh?

Curious, Archer skimmed it:

Dear Lauren,

It certainly hasn't been the same here without you.
The younger girls ask for you nearly every day and
can't wait for your postcards. We're counting the days
until your return...

Footsteps approached, and Archer shoved the note back
into the envelope, heart pounding. She headed back toward
the rec room, mind racing.

What was the Shady Acres Home for Girls?

The rec room bustled with activity, and she half waved to
the Butterflies before ducking into the bathroom off to the
side. There, she leaned against the door and googled "Shady
Acres Home for Girls."

It was a group foster home. Maybe Lauren worked there
or something? But the note had sounded pretty familiar, so...

Archer slid it out and read the whole thing. Her hands
were shaking by the time she finished. She couldn't believe
it—Lauren lived in a foster home.

The strange things about Lauren suddenly clicked: the
way she was ridiculously excited about camp, how she was
so weird about waste, the moments she seemed fascinated by
everyone's families...

Archer sucked in a sharp breath.

What about Lauren's family? Her perfect parents? The
brother?

Lies. All lies.

This letter is going straight back to the mailbox.

Even though she couldn't believe Lauren had lied to them, Archer did not want to reveal her secret. Without her, the Fireflies wouldn't exist.

The thought was too scary for words.

Chapter Twenty-Seven

When Jade walked into her therapy appointment that Friday, the room smelled like Starbucks. Her therapist sipped coffee from an enormous mug.

Jade glared. "I don't want to be here. Just so you know."

For the past two days, the mood in the cabin had been a total bummer. Lauren was still upset about the loss of the scavenger hunt, and Isla had a broken heart. Archer was intermittently upset and then upbeat, which meant she was probably about to do something terrible to Makayla.

The therapist nodded like she knew all about it. "It seems like you might have something on your mind."

"I keep thinking about Catalina," Jade admitted. "Kiara's sister."

Jade didn't mean to say it. She'd done a good job of sitting quietly for the majority of their sessions. But after the nights of depressing silence in the cabin, she was ready to talk.

"Oh?" Instead of picking up a notebook, Mrs. Anderson just sipped her coffee as if they were having a normal conversation.

Jade squinted at the blue pattern on the tissue box. "I think it's because my friend Archer is fighting with her sister. Cat was mean to Kiara, too, but at the end of the day, they were sisters. The fact that Cat killed her—"

"The accident killed her."

Jade paused. "Cat has had a rotten time."

"So have you." The therapist nodded. "Have you reached out to her?"

No. She was terrified.

"You could call her," Mrs. Anderson suggested. "Say what's on your mind?"

How many times had she dialed Kiara's home number during the years of their friendship?

"I can't," Jade whispered. "I wouldn't know what to say."

"How about a letter, then? You wouldn't have to send it, but you could express some of these feelings. What would you say in a letter?"

I'd say I'm sorry. The accident wasn't your fault—it was mine. Kiara looked up to you every day. She always talked about you, wanted to be like you...

The words felt like they came from another place, maybe from Kiara herself.

"Would you like to write a letter?" Mrs. Anderson pressed.

"Is this supposed to be a healing exercise?" she demanded. "Something to make it all better?"

"Do you think writing a letter will make this all better?"

Okay. The woman wasn't as completely clueless as she'd thought.

A yellow legal pad and a pen sat in the corner of the table, just past the magazines.

"I'm using this," Jade said, and settled in to write.

Chapter Twenty-Eight

Time was moving too quickly.

Early morning activities rolled into lunch, which became Indoor Rec, and before Lauren could blink, it was the sixth week of camp. The thought that she could be back again next year, if only the administration said yes, made her feel so happy. Unfortunately, it was hard to be happy when Isla was so sad.

During dinner Monday night, Lauren decided it was time to do something about it.

"I have something to say," she announced.

Archer's forkful of spaghetti stopped halfway to her mouth. "Is it a secret?"

"It's not a secret."

Archer went back to eating. "Well, let me know if you decide to start sharing secrets."

Okay, weird. But sometimes Archer was weird.

Lauren turned to Isla, who was picking at a plate of lemon chicken. "You like Jordan. Sally is sitting right over there. I'm going to find out what happened."

"That's a good idea." Jade gave a serious nod. "It's time."

Isla tried to protest, but Lauren darted away. She returned to the table with the best news ever.

"Isla," Lauren squealed. "They really *are* just friends. Jordan was trying to set her up with Raahithya, that guy in his cabin. He's cool: plays guitar and is supposedly hilarious, but at the scavenger hunt, Raah totally ignored her. She was upset, so Jordan hugged her." Lauren gave Isla a big smile. "But Sally says the only thing he ever talks about is *you*."

Isla put her hand over her heart. "Are you serious? He didn't ask her to the dance?"

"The dance?" Lauren gave her a look of disbelief. "Isla, of course not. He likes *you*."

Isla's face fell. "I ruined it." She threw her arms across the table, wailing. "He'll never talk to me again!"

Lauren had to give it to Isla: for a girl who didn't like attention, she sure knew how to milk her moments.

"He'll talk to you." Lauren rubbed her back. "You just have to apologize."

Isla moaned. "I can't."

"Let's call him." Jade tightened her ponytail. "We have twenty minutes until Cabin Cluster. Let's go right now."

"I can't." Isla shook her head. "I'm too embarrassed."

Lauren grabbed her hand. "Don't you miss him?" she sang.

Isla gave a little smile, and the other Fireflies burst out laughing.

"Okay. I'll call him."

Lauren grinned. This was *exactly* the type of excitement the night needed.

The girls finished up their dinner in two bites and then raced toward the Lodge. Lauren stopped short at the sight of Carol Kennedy walking down the path. "Lauren." She smiled. "Do you have a minute?"

Lauren felt a flash of nerves. "Yes, ma'am. Of course." She waved her friends on. "Go. I'll catch up."

The Fireflies pushed Isla toward the Lodge, giggling, but when Archer looked back over her shoulder, her face was dark.

Does Archer suspect something?

Like most adults, Carol Kennedy started talking about the weather. She called the breeze "lovely," the lake "picturesque," and confessed she "simply adored this type of summer evening." Lauren nodded, squeezing her hands tight.

The weather report complete, Mrs. Kennedy adjusted her glasses. "I have news."

Lauren sucked in a breath. This was it!

The evening sun glinted off the trees, shadows of the leaves practically danced on the ground, and Lauren shivered in anticipation.

"What's the verdict?" she asked.

Mrs. Kennedy let out a tight sigh. "The administration feels that your proposition won't work, for several logistical reasons that would bore you to tears. On another level, however, they also feel it defeats the purpose of camp. Why waste time in the kitchen when you could be having fun and building relationships?"

Lauren stared at her in disbelief. "Why waste time in the kitchen?" Clearly the administration had no concept of her reality.

"Lauren, I do hope that you find a way to return," she continued. "Perhaps you could find a way to pay for the cost of camp while you're back home. You have been a valuable asset to this community, and we look forward to having you return. Now, would you like me to walk with you to meet up with your friends?"

Lauren shook her head. "I'll be fine," she mumbled.

Mrs. Kennedy spotted a counselor. Waving, she cut across the lawn.

The cicadas chirped, and in the distance, a group of campers sang a rhyme while walking down the path. The joyful sounds were so different from the ache Lauren felt inside. Slowly, she sank down onto a nearby bench and put her head in her hands.

The administration thought she could find the resources to return to camp? Please. Even with a job, it would be a challenge to cover the airfare, let alone the cost of camp.

The administrators—everyone—at Blueberry Pine lived in a different world.

You can't be mad at them, though. You knew the score.

Lauren's throat thickened. She wasn't mad at the administration; she was mad at herself for getting her hopes up. Now, she had to face the hurt and heartache of losing people she cared about. Rushing over to the empty doorway of the canteen, she hid her face against the wood and choked back a sob.

When it's over, it's over. I'll never see the other Fireflies again.

Chapter Twenty-Nine

The Fireflies sat on their front porch, enjoying the last minutes of daylight. While Archer struggled to perfect an arm drawing of the cabin cluster, Jade attempted to French braid Isla's hair. It wasn't going well, and the attempt was punctuated by Isla's squeaks.

"Quit pulling," Isla complained.

Jade scolded her in fake French, and the girls giggled.

"There's Lauren." Archer felt relieved to see her walking up the path with Cassandra. She'd been gone for more than an hour and had even missed their group activity.

"Is she okay?" Jade asked.

The girls fell silent, watching them approach.

"Everything's fine," Cassandra called. "Lauren got a little sick after dinner."

Lauren climbed up the steps, looking pale. "Sorry to scare you all." She settled into the chair next to Archer, and Cassandra brought her a bottle of water. "I'm fine, really. What did I miss?"

Archer cringed. "You'll be so mad."

"We worked on a time capsule to open next year," Isla said. "Each cabin included something. We made a jar of origami fireflies out of candy wrappers."

"At least, we *tried* to do that," Jade laughed. "I'm not sure the fireflies are actually identifiable."

Lauren gave a short laugh. "A time capsule. Really?"

The other Fireflies exchanged glances. The activity was so Lauren. She had to be bummed that she missed it.

"I'm sure you could still make a firefly to include," Cassandra suggested. "I could add it to the jar."

Lauren shook her head. "Not a big deal."

Cassandra headed off to chat with one of the other counselors. Once she was out of earshot, Lauren leaned forward. "Isla, what happened with Jordan?"

Isla burst into giggles. "He apologized nearly ten times. I feel so guilty."

"Tell me everything," Lauren squealed.

Archer tuned out. The only romance that interested her was between Paolo and her sister. Earlier, she'd sent Makayla details about the meeting. It was doubtful her sister would question how Paolo knew the camp layout, but Archer had picked a landmark that appeared on the camp website just in case.

I'll be in the woods by the totem pole, the message said. Don't come alone; it's not safe. Bring all your friends. But I will want them to leave at some point. LOL.

The Bluebirds would all be there to see Makayla get stood up and see her heart crushed into smithereens. To top it off,

Archer planned to leave a note on the door of the Bluebirds' cabin, listing all the reasons he ditched.

Pure poetry.

Archer took in her surroundings with a grin. Squirrels darted from tree to tree, birds called to one another, and the setting sun lit the pines with a gentle hue. The forest was made for romance—and total, utter heartbreak.

"What are you smiling about?" Lauren looked at her.

"Trust me, you don't want to know," Archer said.

Jade muttered something in fake French. She had tried to talk Archer out of the plan, but it wasn't working.

Makayla deserved this.

Didn't she?

"Done." Jade pulled Isla to her feet. "What do you guys think?"

The braid wove across Isla's head like a crown, making her look like an actual princess. Archer nearly made a joke, but bit her tongue. Isla had had a long day.

"It looks great," she said, and Lauren nodded.

"Come inside," Jade instructed Isla. "I want you to see it in the mirror."

The screen door creaked shut.

Archer capped her Sharpie. "So, what did the administration lady want?"

Lauren's face clouded over.

"Wait, your eyes are puffy." Archer leaned in. "Have you been crying?"

"Nope. I'm great. So—"

"Hold on. What's going on? Were you actually sick?"

"Shh!" Lauren whispered. "I…" She glanced out across the lawn, where Cassandra was talking with another counselor. "Okay, one of the administrators saw me out walking this morning, and I got a lecture about being alone on the path so early. Don't tell the other girls, okay?"

"They should know if you're upset," Archer scolded. "We're friends."

Lauren waved her hands. "I know, I know. Everyone's been so down, though. Isla was about to make up with Jordan…I didn't want to come back and rain on her parade, you know?"

That made sense. Still, it bugged her how Lauren had tried to act like everything was great. Archer knew not to trust Lauren's words, but now she had to question Lauren's actions too?

I mean…kind of. She lies all the time.

Archer could confront her. But Archer didn't want to do that. For the first time since elementary school, she had a group of friends who didn't judge her. Maybe she shouldn't rush to judge Lauren either.

"Let's go see what Isla thinks of that braid," Lauren said. "Bet she's already taken it out." She grabbed Archer's hands and pulled her up, giggling as they tripped over each other.

Relax. Does it really matter if she's keeping secrets?

It did to Archer.

I want to believe in this whole friends-forever-sisterhood thing.

But if Lauren lied about everything…why would that part be true?

Chapter Thirty

A few days after she'd made up with Jordan, Isla was busy embroidering while the girls got ready for dinner. Archer had been in a foul mood ever since her elective, and was stomping around the cabin. Apparently, someone had found out she was related to Makayla and said, "Your life must be perfect," which had sent her into a tailspin.

"You know what gets me?" Archer straddled a chair. "The fact that anyone would say my life is perfect." She grabbed one of the new Sharpies her mother had included in her care package and went to town on her arm.

Isla could relate. Her life might look perfect from the outside, but now that Jordan was back, she felt so guilty for betraying her parents with a boy. The night before, she'd had a nightmare that they showed up at camp and found her kissing Jordan. It wasn't a terrible dream because of the kissing, but still.

Breaking the rules hadn't mattered so much when Jordan was just a figment of her imagination. Now, though, the relationship was real. It was serious.

It was also completely against their rules.

"My life isn't perfect." Isla pulled the needle through her final stitch and knotted the string. "Nobody's is."

Archer turned to Lauren. "Your life seems perfect, Lauren."

Lauren chewed her upper lip and shrugged.

Isla smiled at her. "You might be the exception." Finished with her work, she stashed the headbands in her kit to ship out later that week.

"Knock, knock." Cassandra walked in with a letter and a package. "You forgot to get the mail."

Cassandra passed a small box to Archer. "If this is candy, don't spoil your dinner. And, Isla, this one's for you."

Isla glanced down. It had a local postmark.

Camp correspondence. Most likely a bill or something I'll have to send to my parents' accountant.

"I've got to run. We're doing a skit at dinner, so don't be late." Cassandra rolled her eyes. "I'll be the one dressed as a dancing cow."

The girls laughed, and Isla opened the envelope. To her surprise, it wasn't a bill. It was a letter written in cramped handwriting on a folded piece of notebook paper.

"You guys!" Isla squealed. "Maybe my life *is* perfect after all." It was from Jordan! In spite of the guilt, it was a thrill to get a letter from him. Especially one like *this*.

Lauren dashed over, grabbed the paper, and read it out loud.

Hi Isla,

I really want to see you again. Do you want to meet me? It's risky, but I think we should do it. Send me back a note and let me know if you and the other Fireflies can meet us at 10:15 p.m. next Monday on the public beach next to the girls' camp. The counselors all have a big bonfire together, so we should have no trouble sneaking out. Let me know.

Love, Jordan

"He signed it 'love,'" Lauren cried. "He signed it 'LOVE'!"

Isla collapsed onto her bed, covering her mouth to hold back hysterical giggles. It was all too exciting for words.

"He wants us to sneak out," she whispered, half worried Cassandra would hear her from somewhere across camp. "I mean…my parents would kill me."

Sneaking out meant walking through the woods to a beach connected to a public campground, which might not be safe. Besides, she could get grounded for life. Perhaps even sent to military school. Meeting him was impossible.

But she wanted to, more than anything in the world.

You can't do this. Stop considering it!

"I could cover for you." Jade picked through Archer's care package until she found a package of Twizzlers. "We could do the pillows-under-blankets routine. I could actually sit up and shush you or something when Cassandra comes back for bed check."

"I can't go alone, though," Isla said.

Lauren raised her hand. "I'll go."

Isla swiped back the letter and brought it to her nose to see if she could smell Jordan.

Jade giggled. "Did you just kiss that?"

"You guys," she cried. "What if he *kisses* me?"

Lauren started singing, "First comes love, then comes marriage..." Archer and Jade made kissing sounds. Once everyone calmed down, Isla got serious.

"Do you really think this is possible?" she asked the girls.

For the first time all night, Archer smiled. "Everything is possible. We're Fireflies."

Chapter Thirty-One

"You're going to have so much fun," Jade told Isla, the night of the big sneak out. "You ready?"

The Fireflies had just returned to Firefly Cabin after a night of Guitar and Ghost Stories. Their hair and clothes smelled like a bonfire, and they'd feasted on s'mores and campfire popcorn. It had been a great night.

Isla gave an eager nod. "I can't wait." She'd never worn makeup before, and earlier, Jade had done her mascara. Her big brown eyes looked gorgeous in the low light.

"Speaking of..." Isla climbed into bed and pulled the pillow over her face. She poked her head back out and said, "You guys, come on. Get into bed."

The other Fireflies exchanged amused glances. Lauren flipped off the lights, and the rest of them climbed into their bunks. They lay in silence for a minute. Then Lauren let out a huff, and the lights were flipped back on.

"Isla." Her whisper rang out across the room. "I'm not super-sure about this."

Jade propped herself up on her elbow in surprise. Lauren paced the room, squeezing her hands like she did when she was nervous.

"This might be a really bad idea," she muttered. "Let's tell him we'll do it tomorrow."

"What?" Isla shot upright. "No, everything is set for tonight. The counselors will be gone. We have to do it tonight."

"It's just..." Lauren's voice trailed off.

"What?" Jade pressed.

Archer started laughing. "The relay race is tomorrow. Lauren doesn't want to mess it up."

Isla's mouth dropped open. "You can't be serious."

"That's not the reason," Lauren said. "Now that you bring it up, though, am I the only one in this cabin who thinks the competition is important? Because it's starting to seem that way."

"Excuse me, I sang in front of people." Isla was clearly offended. "My commitment should be pretty clear."

"And I would give away an entire year's worth of candy to beat my sister," Archer insisted. "So please don't say that again."

"Lauren, you're faster than anyone at camp," Jade reminded her. "Sleep or no sleep, we have a really good shot. Besides, you promised."

Even though Jade didn't want to upset Lauren, she did think Isla deserved this experience. Isla liked Jordan so much. This was her chance to really spend some time with him, and maybe he'd even ask her to be his date to the coed dance.

"Please, Lauren," Isla said. "You promised."

Moths pinged against the screen. Outside, the fire hissed as the counselors doused it with water. Smoke wafted in through the window, and Isla gave a pathetic cough.

Lauren sighed, switched off the lights, and climbed back into her bunk. "Okay, fine."

"Time for bed," Cassandra called, banging open the screen door. "Goodness! You guys must be tired."

"Or terrified," Archer said cheerfully. "That story about the headless man was epic. Thanks for traumatizing us."

Cassandra laughed. "Thanks. I do my best. Night, all." The moment she was gone, Isla darted for the door. Lauren hesitated but followed.

Loons called on the lake, their mournful cry echoing in the night. Jade flipped on her flashlight and pulled out an envelope.

The morning after she'd written the apology letter to Cat, she'd mailed it on a whim. She'd never expected to hear back, but had received a response that afternoon. The unopened envelope had sat under her pillow for a few hours, but each time she considered reading it, panic squeezed her heart. Now, she stared at the springs on the bed above her, breathing deeply and wondering what it said.

Fireflies flashed outside the window, and mosquitoes buzzed against the screen. She hesitated, turning the envelope over and over in her hands.

Should I read it?

"Don't judge me," said a voice, close to her ear.

Jade jumped. Archer lurked next to the bed, her eyes bright and manic.

"Paolo is meeting Makayla tonight."

No. No, no, no.

"If I'm not back in time, you'll have to cover for everybody."

"I don't like this," Jade said.

It was so mean. Yes, Makayla was awful, but she also seemed hopelessly insecure.

"Archer, a prank is one thing, but I don't understand how you could hurt her like that. Deliberately."

"My sister is evil," Archer insisted.

"Look..." Jade let out a deep breath. "Kiara was like your sister. Beautiful, and yes, she could be really mean. But, Archer, English was her second language, and she barely spoke in elementary school. The other girls made fun of her. Once she learned to stand up for herself, she was not about to get bullied again."

Archer scoffed. "My sister has never stopped talking, so I think we're good."

"You're missing the point," Jade groaned. "I'm trying to say you never know why people act the way they do."

"*You're* missing the point. My sister deserves this."

"Nobody deserves this." Jade glared at her. "You're my friend, so I can say this: grow up, Archer."

Archer glared back. "Will you cover for me or not?"

I should say no.

Like that would make a difference. This was a mistake Archer was determined to make.

"Fine. But I know you're going to regret it."

Archer mumbled something and stomped out.

Jade sat in silence for several minutes. The trees seemed to sigh in the night air. It was so quiet, she could hear the hum of the overhead fan.

Letting out a slow breath, she took Cat's letter out of the envelope. The handwriting was so familiar. Jade squinted, leaning in.

Dear Jade,

I was so surprised to get your letter. I was scared to read it, honestly, and afraid you would say the accident was my fault. Why didn't I drive slower? Why didn't I steer the car away from the tree? Those questions haunt me every day. The fact that you wrote to say you were sorry? I never expected that.

I can't believe you blame yourself. Kiara told me some of the things she said to you that night, and I want you to know something: she felt terrible.

Jade froze. She had to read the sentence three times before she could continue.

She begged me to take her back to your house, but by then, the snow was coming down hard. I wouldn't do it because the roads were getting bad. Can you believe it? If I had turned back, everything would be different. But if you have any doubt in your mind about how Kiara felt about you, know this: she loved you like a sister.

You were such a good friend to her. Thank you for getting in touch. When you get back from camp, I would very much like to see you.

Abrazos y besos,
Cat

Jade didn't know how long she sat in silence, staring at the letter. She touched her cheeks, surprised to discover they were damp with tears. Bringing the letter to her heart, she let out loud, choking sobs.

Kiara had wanted to come back to her house! They would have been friends again by midnight.

Jade read the letter at least five times, then laid down and stared up at the mattress springs. Finally, she sat up and looked at the clock. It couldn't have been more than fifteen minutes since Archer left.

You were such a good friend to her, Cat said.

Jade climbed out of bed and found a black sweater.

I am a good friend. It's time to be a good friend again.

She snuck out of the cabin.

Chapter Thirty-Two

Archer hid behind a tree, watching her sister.

Makayla stood in the clearing, fidgeting with her heart-shaped Tiffany necklace and pouting with her glossy lips. The Bluebirds whispered to one another. Two of the girls seemed to be getting bored.

"Maybe he's not coming," one finally said.

Makayla shot her a deadly look. "Oh, baby's tired? Then go back to the cabin."

Something crashed through the brush, and all the girls, including Archer, stood up straight. The sound faded into the night, and the Bluebirds nervously giggled. They started telling ghost stories, and eventually, Makayla sat down on one of the large logs with them, looking bummed out.

It's getting to her. She's about to lose it...

"I'm cold." She jumped up. "Obviously, he got stuck in Detroit and sent a message at the last minute. He doesn't know I'm living in the third world and can't check the Internet every second of the day."

Wow. Makayla didn't bring her phone to camp?

That made Archer feel cooler somehow.

"Do you want to go back?" asked the short girl who was always with her. Quickly, she added, "We'll stay as long as you want."

Makayla stretched. "No, let's go. I'm sure he'll try again tomorrow, so we better get some rest."

To Archer's absolute delight, the other two Bluebirds exchanged glances like, *Yeah, right.* They probably doubted Makayla had a boyfriend at all, which was hilarious.

The Bluebirds filed through the woods. Archer trailed them, heart pounding.

Just wait until they see the note…

It was tacked on the door of the cabin and said: "You look nothing like your picture. I saw you in the forest and I am repulsed. I am a model and only date beautiful girls. You seem like the type who might look okay on the outside, but is covered with warts within…"

The note went on and on. It was *so* mean, and Archer felt a rush of glee. It was time someone taught her sister a lesson. Maybe Makayla would finally learn it was not okay to hurt other people.

But isn't that what you're doing?

Fine. Yes, but she was proving a point! This wasn't the time to have doubts.

Archer chewed her nails, and memories started flipping through her head: baking brownies with Makayla, sneaking downstairs early on Christmas morning, sharing clothes before her sister was all into designer brands...

The memories got darker.

She thought of those moments her sister had broken down—when her pet bunny died or the time she didn't get invited to a big party in elementary school. Back then, Makayla had tried so hard to keep up with the older girls in their neighborhood.

The memory of her sister as a sad and lonely kid was unexpected. Back then, Archer would have done anything to protect her.

So, why am I trying so hard to hurt her now?

Jade's words jumped into her head: *It's easy to judge someone by how they look, but you never know what people are going through.*

A chill cut through her.

I can't do this.

But there was no way to stop it.

You have to.

Archer darted through the trees, desperate to beat the Bluebirds to their cabin. Branches slashed at her face, and she burst into the clearing at the edge of the forest. To her horror, the Bluebirds were already at the cabin steps.

She hung back in the trees, feeling sick.

I'm sorry, Makayla. I'm so sorry...

The cabin door banged shut. Had they grabbed the note and gone inside?

She felt a hand on her shoulder and whirled around.

Jade.

"You were so right." Archer practically fell into her arms. "I took it too far."

Jade hugged her tight. "It's okay."

"It's not okay." Archer's voice cracked. "I can't take it back. I—"

Jade held up a piece of paper. "It never happened."

The note. Jade had the note!

Archer grabbed it out of her hands. Yes, this was it. But how…

"I took it before they got back." Jade's blue eyes shined in the dark night. "She never even saw it."

Too many emotions whirled inside Archer to process. Humiliation, relief, confusion…then absolute fury.

"How dare you?" she hissed.

Jade blinked. "Huh?"

"This was *my* problem, not yours."

"Archer." Jade grabbed the note and wadded it up. "Be happy it's over."

Happy? How could she be happy?

Look at what she'd done. Makayla might be mean, but now, there was no doubt: Archer was even worse.

Tears streamed down her face, and she took off running, desperate to escape the person she'd become.

Chapter Thirty-Three

The moment Isla saw Jordan standing on the beach, the moon-light glinting off his dark hair, the world seemed perfect. He kicked off his shoes, and giggling, she did the same.

"Hi." He took her hand. "You look beautiful. Let's go for a walk."

The night felt enchanted. Mist swirled above the water, and stars glittered like fireflies overhead.

"I can't believe you wanted to do this," she said, looking up at him as they strolled along the shore.

"It's so risky." He grinned. "Do you know how much trouble we'd get into? We'd make history as the worst campers ever."

"The ones who ruined it for everyone." She felt bold making jokes like Archer. "It's worth it, though. To spend time with you."

He stopped and looked at her. They stood in silence for what felt like three hours. Then he leaned forward and placed his lips against hers.

With a shiver, she wrapped her arms around his neck. Her head spun at the warmth of his mouth. A million thoughts ran through her mind:

My parents are going to kill *me!*

Am I doing this right?

Wow, he smells good.

I love him.

The first thought kept coming back, though. Her parents would be horrified. Not only had she disobeyed them, but they had never even met the boy she was kissing.

In her heart, Isla knew her mother would have wanted to shop together to find the perfect outfit for Isla's first date. Her father would have wanted to meet Jordan at the front door, shake his hand, and grill him about politics in the library. Both of her parents would have watched with pride as he took her arm and escorted her to the elevator like a gentleman. Instead, she was sneaking around, and the guilt was totally interfering.

Don't think about it. Think about him.

Jordan hugged her close.

"Let's sit."

He guided her through the sand to a piece of driftwood. It was damp and cold of course, but Isla was getting used to the pitfalls of nature. Besides, Jordan was there to keep her warm.

The full moon rose in the sky as they talked. They touched on serious topics like school and their parents. Isla told him how strict her parents were, but did not reveal that she would need permission to date him. The thought was too depressing, so thank goodness he made her laugh, joking about his counselor and the other guys in his cabin. He was so smart, so quick-witted, that Isla couldn't help but think: *My parents will like him. I know they will.*

"I found a copy of the song you sang," he said suddenly. "I listened to it, like, a hundred times. You sound better than the singer." Before she could respond, he added, "Still, I know someone who can sing it better than you."

Jordan leaped to his feet and let out a warbling cry. He started dancing in silly, jerky moves and pulled Isla to her feet. He led her across the sand, and she laughed until her sides hurt.

Isla was having so much fun that she didn't notice the warning signs until it was too late. She stopped abruptly and put her hand to her chest. Her lungs were tight, and her breath, thick.

She was having an asthma attack.

With a start, she realized she hadn't even thought to transfer her inhaler from her uniform to her black shorts. The telltale sound of a wheeze escaped her lips, and she plunked down on the nearest log. Sweat dampened her neck as her mind went into a singular focus point of survival.

Jordan was still laughing from their ridiculous dancing. He bopped over to her, stretching out his hands. "Come on. You've got more moves than that!"

The wheeze came louder now, thicker.

"I can't." She was too scared to be embarrassed. "I can't breathe."

His expression turned serious. "What?"

"I have asthma," she said in short bursts. "I forgot my inhaler in the cabin, but there's not enough time to get it. I'm going to need an ambulance."

The gravity of the situation hit her. Everyone would get caught. Her parents would know she had been on the beach with a boy in the middle of the night.

What was she *thinking*? Why had she thought she could get away with this?

"I didn't know you had asthma," Jordan said.

Now was *not* the time to play getting-to-know-you.

"Go," Isla gasped. "Get help."

"Okay, but..." He rummaged through his pockets and pulled out a blue contraption. "I know it's not yours." He held it out. "But I take this in emergencies. Use it and I'll get help."

Isla stared at him in disbelief.

Jordan has the same inhaler as I do.

He has asthma.

He is perfect.

Isla grabbed the inhaler and took two greedy puffs. It cut through the fog with a minty, medicinal taste. She felt the small branches of her lungs open and oxygen reenter her bloodstream.

Jordan was already jogging down the beach, toward the path.

"Wait!" she shouted.

He turned, his silhouette lanky in the pale light of the moon. "I have to get help!"

"No, you don't," she called. "It worked. We have the same inhaler."

Jordan let out a cheer. He jogged back, sat on the log, and pulled her into the crook of his arm. "I knew that stupid thing would be good for something. When did you get asthma?"

Isla never dreamed she would share this with anyone, let alone the boy of her dreams. It turned out Jordan got asthma when he was in fifth grade too.

"It's so embarrassing. I've been hiding it from the girls this whole time."

Jordan looked confused. "Why? They're not your friends if you can't tell them things that matter."

Isla looked down at her hands. The other Fireflies *were* her friends. There was no reason to keep secrets from them. It was just...

"I feel ashamed about it," she admitted.

Jordan frowned. "Why? Lots of kids have asthma."

"No one in *my* family. My older brothers are perfect. They're so smart and so sporty. Even my grandmother runs marathons, and she's seventy-something. My parents seem bewildered by my asthma, as if I'm a science experiment gone wrong."

"Even more reason to tell your friends," Jordan said. "They won't think it's weird. They would probably even help you through all that."

It *was* hard to imagine Lauren making fun of her for having asthma. Or any of the girls, really.

"You might be right. I'll...try." She looked up at the moon and then, feeling bold, leaned her head against his shoulder. "Thank you for saving my life."

"I wanted to give you a reason to like me," Jordan joked.

Isla grabbed his face and kissed him.

Chapter Thirty-Four

The white sand glowed in the silver light of the moon. Jordan had brought two of his friends: the blond boy who'd been with him outside at the singing competition, and Raahithya, the one Sally liked. The second Jordan and Isla headed down the beach, the guys stripped off their shirts and jumped into the lake for a night swim, leaving Lauren alone.

In the moonlight, she could see Isla and Jordan sitting on a log by the water. It made her happy that Isla was happy, but it felt dangerous being at the beach at all. It was a risk she didn't like taking.

If they got caught, they would get sent home. That meant no more campfires, no more competition, and no more Fireflies.

You're here now, though. So, enjoy it.

Letting out a breath, Lauren got to her feet. "I'm going to take a walk," she called to Jordan's cabinmates, but they didn't notice.

Lauren walked up along the edge of the trees. It was a beautiful night, and the stars were nearly as bright as the moon. She had started to feel better about things, since she'd accepted camp was only a temporary situation. Still, it wasn't easy, because the experience had changed her.

For example, she finally knew what it was like to play in a sports league. She could kick a soccer goal or shoot baskets with the best of them. It seemed hopelessly unfair, all of a sudden, to think she wouldn't be able to play back at school.

Life is not fair.

Lauren knew that, coming in. But somewhere along the way, the lines had gotten blurred, and she'd thought she could make this experience last forever.

Lesson learned. Now, she had to bite her tongue every time the girls tried to plan for next year: What snacks should Archer bring? Should they draw straws for top or bottom bunk, to keep it fair? What cabin would they get?

The girls would be disappointed to have someone take her place, she did know that. They would move on, though, and forget her. The thought hurt, which was frustrating. People didn't stick around—she'd learned that early on—so why had she let herself get attached to these girls?

You have to let them go. When it's over, it's over. There's no point in hanging on. Lauren returned to the edge of the water, pulled her knees to her chest, and waited.

* * *

Jordan's friends emerged from the water, wet and shivering.

"We gotta get back," Raahithya said. "I'm gonna go grab him."

"I'll do it." Lauren jumped to her feet and raced down the sand, relieved the night was finally over. "We should head back," she called.

The second the words were out of her mouth, she tripped on something. A root, a piece of driftwood—she had no idea, but there was a sudden pop and a burst of pain. She dropped with a yelp.

Jordan was at her side in an instant. "What happened? You okay?"

Pain ripped through her ankle. It hurt like a thousand little pinpricks but then subsided.

"I'm fine. I just stepped on something wrong."

"Phew." Isla giggled. "I would be grounded for life if we had to call for an ambulance."

Lauren's mouth dropped open. Uh, what about the fact that she could have been seriously injured? Wouldn't that be greater cause for concern?

Stop, you're just tired.

"Can you walk back?" Jordan asked.

"I think." Lauren tried to take a few steps. It hurt a little bit to walk, but it wasn't a big deal. "Really, I'm fine."

Jordan and Isla smiled at each other, and his friends approached.

"Come on," the blond said. "The canoe express is leaving."

The group marched across the silvery beach, and Isla said her final goodbye to Jordan.

Lauren and Isla slipped into the forest in silence. Lauren

focused on putting one foot in front of the other and not tripping on anything else.

"Don't you want to ask how it went?" Isla sounded hurt.

"Not at the moment." Every step she took hurt a little bit more. "I just want to make it back home."

"Does your ankle still hurt?" Isla asked.

Lauren let out a huff. "Do you even care?"

"Lauren!" Isla stopped walking. "Of course I care! Is that what you think?"

Lauren stopped too. In an angry whisper, she said, "You were more worried about not getting grounded than making sure I was okay!"

"No, I…" Isla shook her head. "It's a long story. Let's talk about it in the morning."

"Fine by me," Lauren grumbled.

They reached Blueberry Pine's stretch of beach, and Lauren hobbled along in silence. The closer they got to camp, the more worried she became that Cassandra would be waiting for them. She froze at every hoot of an owl or crack of a tree branch in the wind. Finally, they reached the path leading to the cabin, snuck up the steps, and slipped inside.

Cassandra's cot was still empty, which meant the bonfire was going strong. They were safe.

Jade rubbed her eyes. "How did it go?" she asked groggily.

Lauren climbed into bed and pulled a pillow over her face. "We're going to lose the race."

* * *

Lauren gritted her teeth. Her ankle burned, her breath came in short gasps, but there were only five girls in front of her. The red ribbon for the finish line stretched across the sand.

You can do it. Push yourself.

For a split second, she did. Her legs propelled her forward, and her heart pounded like an Olympic athlete's. But no matter how hard she pushed, she couldn't get past the warning pain in her ankle.

Come on. Go!

Too late. Dana, one of the Cardinals, crashed through the red ribbon and took first.

Lauren ran through and collapsed, trying to catch her breath. She rolled onto her back and stretched out her leg. The sun was about a thousand degrees, and she was sticky with sweat and sand. Her ankle hurt, but at least it hadn't snapped halfway through.

"Great job, Lauren!" Isla's tiny voice was punctuated by applause.

Lauren cracked open an eye. The other Fireflies stood over her, dark silhouettes against the sun. Somewhere by the finish line, the Cardinals cheered, accepting their trophy.

"I need a shower," she muttered, brushing sand off her legs.

Isla, Archer, and Jade exchanged glances.

"Look, we did great," Jade said. "That wasn't easy."

The race had been a combination of boating, baton passing, and obstacle courses. "We came in sixth," she added, "so we'll get some points."

Isla nodded. "We're still in the running."

Barely. The Cardinals came in first, and the Bluebirds, second. That meant the Fireflies were neck and neck with both of them.

"We would have won if we hadn't gone last night," Lauren said.

The sound of a whistle cut through the air. "Campers, it's mealtime!" Taylor shouted into her bullhorn. "Mush, mush."

"Saved by the bell," Isla said, grinning.

Lauren gritted her teeth. Since when did Isla make snappy little jokes? Oh, right. Since the girl who had everything got a boyfriend too.

Stop! You can't think that way. The group walked to the mess hall in silence. The thick smell of tomato sauce cut through the air. Chicken parmigiana—it smelled good, but too heavy for the hot day. Still, Chef must have worked hard on it, so Lauren stood in line while the other Fireflies headed for other things.

The campers next to her chattered with excitement, recapping the race. It seemed like everyone had had a great time.

Except me.

Chef waved at her from the kitchen, and Lauren forced a smile.

Jade, Archer, and Isla stopped talking when she arrived at the table. They must have been talking about her. Irritated, Lauren looked down at her tray.

It was packed full. Chicken parmigiana, green beans,

garlic bread, and a small piece of Italian cake. She wasn't even hungry, but she planned to eat every bite, out of respect for Chef. The other girls clearly didn't care about that.

Jade's plate was loaded with fresh fruit and cottage cheese from the salad bar. Isla had the chicken, but had skipped the bread, dessert, and green beans in favor of a limp green salad. Archer was eating cereal for lunch.

Cereal.

Lauren couldn't imagine skipping a hot meal for Fruity Pebbles. Letting out a slow breath, she looked out at the lake, remembering the way she'd sat in the sand and waited for Isla the night before. She took a furious bite, tomato sauce sour on her tongue.

Silence hung over the table. The only sound was Archer slurping her milk. Finally, Lauren slammed down her fork.

"Why are you eating cereal for lunch?" she demanded. "Eat a meal!"

"Huh?" Archer stopped mid-chew. "When did you become the food police?"

Jade held up her hands. "Hey. I think we're all a little tired..."

Archer tipped her bowl back to drink her milk, but not before saying, "Here comes the peacemaker."

Jade drew back. "Excuse me?"

"You heard me." Archer shot Jade a look from behind extra-thick eyeliner. "It's not your job to try and fix everything."

"Somebody has to." Isla gave a delicate cough. "Since you couldn't be bothered to help cover last night."

"Uh, if we'd stayed in the cabin, none of this would have happened," Lauren argued. "I told you something—"

"Enough already!" Archer's spoon clanked against the bowl. "I, I, I. That's all anyone thinks about around here."

"That's rich," Jade muttered. "Considering the only thing we've heard about all summer is *your* sister. I can count the times on one hand you've asked me what I'm going through."

Archer's face turned so red it could have caught on fire. "I didn't need to ask. You're Miss Woe Is Me every second of the day."

Okay, this was getting bad.

"You know what?" Lauren picked up her fork, regretting the fact that her bad mood had started all of this. "You're right. We're all a little tired…"

"No!" Archer slammed her hands onto the table. "I'm not *tired*. I'm mad. But the only thing you care about is being able to look at yourself on the camp website."

Lauren froze. Is *that* what Archer thought?

"I want to be the faces of Blueberry Pine to have a memory of the best summer of my life and the best friends I ever had. Maybe that doesn't include you."

"Maybe not." Archer crossed her arms. "I might not have a lot of friends, but the ones I do have don't lie to me."

Lauren's blood turned cold. "What do you mean?"

Archer held Lauren's gaze. For a world-crumbling moment, Lauren feared she knew her secret—and that she was about to tell it. Instead, Archer got to her feet.

"I mean this whole Firefly-friends-for-life thing is a pile of crap." Her heavy black eyeliner couldn't hide the hurt in her eyes. "How can we be friends if we're not there for one another? You know, I wasted my birthday wish on being friends with you guys forever. I'd like to change that now. I'd like to wish we'd never met."

Turning, she stomped away.

Lauren gripped her tray. "We are friends," she whispered. "We just..."

"Don't like one another?" Jade said. "Yeah, I got that." She took off.

Isla's face crumpled.

Lauren sat in silence. Then she set her jaw, turned her attention to her plate, and focused on eating every last bite of her meal.

Chapter Thirty-Five

Archer stomped through camp. The air was fresh from the rain that morning, and campers laughed in the distance. Her jaw ached from fighting back tears.

Make it to the art building. Then you can hide behind an easel and cry.

The building smelled deep and musty like clay. She'd miss that back home, just like she'd thought she'd miss the Fireflies.

But that was over.

For the last two weeks of camp, she would spend as little time with her cabinmates as possible, especially know-it-all Jade.

"Hey." Archer gave an awkward nod to the counselor at the front desk. It wasn't annoying Mallory, thank goodness, but the artsy girl with the pixie cut and a diamond nose ring.

"Be right back." The girl headed for the back room and returned with Archer's painting.

It was only back there because Jade had stuck her nose into the situation and asked the counselors to keep Archer's work in the office. It was so embarrassing. She never would have said a thing; she would have just dealt with it, like always.

Wiping sweat off the back of her neck, she studied the canvas—a painting of her house back home. Before the incident last night, she'd started the painting so her parents would frame it and hang it in the living room, which would annoy Makayla. Now, she didn't know what to do with it.

Dipping the brush into the paint, Archer touched up the tree branches outside the window of Makayla's room. It reminded her of the countless nights Makayla had snuck out the window to visit her popular friends. Archer would watch, terrified, as her sister walked down their suburban block by herself, the streetlights casting a halo over her head.

Those nights, Archer had counted the hours until her sister came home, paranoid about what might happen to Makayla. Until one night, when she was angry and had locked the window so Makayla couldn't get back inside.

It was winter. She knew Makayla would rather freeze to death than wake their parents. When Archer had heard her sister rattle the window, she'd darted back in and undone the lock. Archer fell asleep crying, worried what could have happened if she'd fallen asleep and left her outside.

Like last night.

If Jade had not stepped in…

But she had.

This morning at the relay race, Makayla had been visibly upset. She didn't have on any makeup—highly unusual—and her spark was gone. The Bluebirds had cheered and chanted while she stared out at the lake, probably nursing heartbreak or hope that things would still work out with Paolo.

I bet she wrote to him.

The thought hit Archer with a start. It hadn't even crossed her mind that her sister would reach out to him. Now, as certain as the blue, red, and yellow vials of paint would give her the colors of the rainbow, she knew there would be a message on her phone.

"I have to run back to the cabin for a minute," she told the counselor. "Can I leave my painting up?"

The counselor looked at the clock. "No worries."

Archer sprinted to Firefly Cabin. It was empty, and she felt a pang at how strange it seemed now. Feeling like an intruder, she climbed to the top of her bunk and pulled out her phone.

There was a message.

Reception was spotty, and it took ages to pull up, but it finally did.

Dear Paolo,

I don't know how to explain how hurt I was that you didn't show up last night. Maybe you got stuck at the photo shoot? I really need to see you. You're the first person in years I've been able to really talk to. Everyone else is so fake—me included, I guess—because no one knows the real me but you. All this to say that I count the seconds until I hear from you, because...and I was going to tell you this last night...I love you.

Your M.

Archer put her hand to her heart. She couldn't have imagined her snotty, aloof sister saying those words, but there they were, in black and white.

Immediately, Archer started to type:

Makayla,

I'm sorry I didn't

Archer stopped.

Enough. I have to tell her.

She fell back against her pillow, her heart sick with fear. What was the alternative? Keep the charade going for the next few years?

Jade was right: it was cowardly, and it was cruel. Makayla thought she'd found someone who understood her, but it was all a big lie.

The agony of last night shot through Archer, followed by the terror she'd felt the night she locked her sister out in the snow. Was that the person she wanted to be?

It's time to grow up, Jade had said.

I don't know how to do that.

Really, though, she did. She had to talk to Makayla.

Chapter Thirty-Six

Isla sat in a corner of the Lodge. The black nail polish Archer had loaned her was chipped. Yesterday, it had seemed so edgy, but today, it just made her hands look dirty.

It's not me. Like everything lately.

The past few weeks had been so strange. Camp felt like a pass to do anything she wanted, but she had taken it too far.

Wearing makeup, sneaking out, kissing a boy...What was I thinking?

Isla had almost died, and Lauren got hurt. Then instead of apologizing...

I acted like a spoiled brat.

Someone tapped her shoulder. She looked up, hoping it was a Firefly.

"Phone call," Cassandra said.

Isla braced herself as she'd walked to the phone. Her parents? Did they somehow know that she'd betrayed their trust?

"Hello?"

"Hello, beautiful," said a warm voice.

Jordan.

Isla wrapped the phone cord around her wrist. "Hi."

"I wanted to check on Lauren. And you."

Isla tightened the cord. "Lauren is fine. We lost the race so she's kind of mad, but she's fine."

Jordan laughed. "Isla, I had so much fun with you last night. When can we do it again?"

This was excruciating.

She liked him so much, but her first kiss should have been one of the best experiences of her life. Instead, she felt sick with guilt.

"I can't." She released the cord. "I can't see you again."

"What? *Why?*"

She sank down to the floor, not caring in the slightest that it was dirty. "Jordan, my parents won't let me date until I'm fifteen."

"Fifteen?" He let out a sound like an injured animal. "That's, like, ancient!"

"I know." She studied her nails, hating the chipped polish more and more.

"There's the dance, though," Jordan pleaded. "Can I at least see you then?"

Isla rested her forehead against the wall. "I can't go. Cassandra told me my parents didn't sign the permission form."

"You could ask them," he insisted. "See if they'll change their minds."

"I'll ask. If they say yes, you'll see me there. It's doubtful, though."

Jordan went silent for what felt like an eternity. "Isla Meyers," he finally said. "You really know how to play hard to get."

She blushed, remembering the feeling of his lips on hers. Even though she wanted to see him more than anything, she had to stop breaking the rules. The guilt was too much to handle.

"Thank you for calling, Jordan. I'll never forget last night."

Once they hung up, she waited for tears. Instead, she felt relieved that she had been honest. That she had done the right thing.

Lifting her chin, Isla walked out to the lobby. She needed to borrow some nail polish remover. More than that, she needed to find her friends.

Chapter Thirty-Seven

Jade whipped a stone at the lake. It plunked into the water.

These girls forced me to be their friend. Now, they're going to let Firefly Cabin fall apart?

She whipped another stone.

Kiara had left a void Jade could never fill. But the Fireflies had helped. She had opened up to them—to Archer, in particular. How could they destroy that?

The thought made her scoop up a handful of stones and throw them in a rage. *Plunk, plunk, plunk,* skip-skip-skip-skip-skip.

She stopped short.

Five times. The stone had skipped *five times.*

"Shut *up.*" She looked around to see if anyone had seen.

Nope. The beach was empty.

Digging through the sand, Jade unearthed another skipping stone. Flat like Archer had taught her. Then she winged it at the water.

Skip-skip-skip-skip-skip.

Five skips, again! She wanted to rush in and tell the girls, but after what had happened—

What had happened, exactly?

The Fireflies had a fight.

"That was all it was," Jade whispered.

Her heart started to pound.

One day, the therapist had said, *everything will stop feeling like the end of the world.*

They'd had a *fight*. So what? It *didn't* have to be the end of the world!

She could put the Fireflies back together. If there was a chance to fix things, she wanted to try.

Jade rushed toward the art building and ran to the back room.

Archer was painting a house on a snowy street. It was so detailed, Jade could imagine living there.

"You are too talented for words."

Archer spun around, the paintbrush out like a sword. She held Jade's gaze for a moment, then turned back to the piece. Her shoulders were squared in that defensive, tough-girl posture that meant she was hurting inside.

"It's a work in progress," Archer mumbled.

Jade sighed. "You know, I would be your number one fan if you weren't such a problem peacock."

"A problem peacock?" Archer turned to glower. "What does that even mean?"

For a moment, it seemed Jade's attempt at humor had backfired. Then Archer burst out laughing in that ridiculous staccato guffaw.

"A problem peacock?" she repeated. "That's, like, the dumbest thing I've ever heard."

Jade giggled. "Look, I want to say I'm sorry. I shouldn't have interfered."

"Yeah, you should have." Archer looked at her boots. "I was just so embarrassed. I couldn't believe I'd done something so heinous."

Jade nodded. "But it's over."

"No. I still have to tell Makayla about Paolo."

Wow. That's unexpected.

"I'm scared." Archer blew a strand of hair out of her face. "Things could get so much worse."

"I'll be there," Jade said. "You're stuck with me."

Archer blinked back tears. "That's the best news I've heard all day."

Chapter Thirty-Eight

Lauren curled up on a couch and pretended to watch the movie so she could hide her swollen eyes. The campers sitting nearby couldn't know that she was heartbroken.

For weeks, she'd struggled with the fact that she would have to say goodbye to her friends at the end of the summer. She hadn't thought she might lose them before that, and now their friendship was over. Because in spite of her best intentions, she had still harbored anger and resentment toward the other Fireflies about things that were not their fault.

I was so selfish.

Lauren bit her lip, thinking of how rude she'd been, making such a big deal about sneaking out. Yes, they could have gotten caught, but hadn't *she* suggested the night swim? How was that any different? She'd been petty and mean, when Isla had been nothing but sweet, vulnerable, and such a good friend.

Then there was Archer.

Lauren had lashed out at her for eating cereal! In truth, Lauren loved the fact that Archer did whatever she felt like, without worrying about the consequences. Archer was bold, brash, and had taught Lauren so much about how to be an individual.

Not to mention Jade.

When camp started, she had been shrouded in loss. But Jade had fought back against her sorrow to show them she was mischievous and kind. Lauren had learned a ton from her about making the best of a bad situation.

These girls are my heroes. I need them in my life.

Lauren had just made the decision to go find them and beg for forgiveness when she felt a sharp tap on her shoulder. She turned, and her heart jumped to see Jade, Archer, and Isla.

"Can we talk to you?" Jade whispered.

Was it possible that they still wanted to be friends?

Lauren got to her feet and shook out her right foot, which had gone numb. The girls clustered together in the corner of the room.

Jade stepped forward. "We wanted to say we're sorry."

"You were right." Isla nodded. "We never should have gone to the beach. It was a terrible idea."

"And I failed you guys." Archer looked down at her boots. "Not cool."

"I love you girls," Jade said. "Please, can we stay friends?"

Lauren's eyes filled with tears. Could it be possible that it wasn't over?

It will be, though. In less than two weeks. You'll have to deal with this heartache all over again.

Lauren squared her shoulders. So what? They could stay in touch. It might not be the same, but she would not lose them.

Tentatively, Archer put her hand out for the secret handshake.

"Lauren, bring it in?" Jade pressed.

Lauren hesitated. "You guys mean so much to me."

"I second that," Archer said. "More than you'll ever know."

"I third it," Jade said.

"Fourths." Isla nodded.

The Fireflies put their hands in the center and bounced them up and down. Lauren felt a smile light up her heart. As loud as she could, she cried, "Zap, zap, zap" and relished in the image of a firefly lighting up the darkness.

Chapter Thirty-Nine

Archer put off talking to Makayla for three days, but when she finished her painting, she knew it was time.

"It's done?" Jade rushed over. "Perfect. Your parents will love it."

They *would* be pretty stoked. The painting had turned out better than she'd expected. It might even make her mom cry.

"Yeah, but…" She brushed her fingers across the branches of the tree outside Makayla's window. "I kept telling myself that when this was done, I'd talk to my sister."

Jade's eyes went big.

"So…right now?" she whispered.

Archer looked at the clock. There was an hour left of Indoor Rec. The Fireflies had planned to trick Makayla and lock her in one of the storage rooms, so Archer could talk to her in private.

Archer gave a grim nod. "Let's do it."

* * *

Archer hid in the room, doodling on her arm. The door rattled and Makayla flounced in.

"Wait, my counselor isn't in—" Makayla started to say.

Lauren slammed the door shut.

"Hey!" Makayla shrieked.

Archer held her phone's flashlight under her chin. "Boo."

Makayla's face contorted with rage. "What do you think you're doing?"

Archer kicked a chair forward like something out of a cop show. "Take a seat."

The words that Makayla unleashed would have gotten her grounded for six months. She kicked at the door, but it didn't matter. The other Fireflies were outside, clapping and chanting to block out the sound.

"Let me out of here right now," Makayla hissed, "or you will regret it."

"Relax." Archer sounded calm, but inside, she was shaking. "Here." She held out a can of cherry Coke. "Drink this and listen."

Cherry Coke was her sister's favorite. They had begged Chef to pick some up from town. Makayla would be desperate for one by now.

Makayla's eyes settled on the can. She wore silver sparkle eyeliner and a dramatic, dark shadow that looked really good.

"Your makeup looks cool," Archer tried.

"Your hair looks stupid," Makayla shot back.

Uggh.

"Look." Archer straddled a chair. "I have something to tell you: I'm Paolo."

Makayla froze. "What are you *talking* about?"

Archer held up her iPhone. "I made him up. I am so, so sorry." So many times during the past year, she'd imagined this moment with triumph. Now, she felt nothing but shame. "It was a joke at first, but then..." She ducked her head, embarrassed. "I liked hearing from you. Your thoughts, your feelings..."

Makayla looked horrified. "You are an absolute psycho."

Archer was worried that was true. But Jade had already assured her that, no, she wasn't a psycho. She was just a girl who'd made a huge mistake.

The chair squeaked as Archer kicked her boots against the floor. She nearly apologized again, but then, Makayla grabbed the cherry Coke. The can hissed as she popped it open.

"I knew he was too good to be true," she muttered.

"I know." Archer nodded. "I have felt so guilty..."

"You're really going to sit here and talk about yourself?" Makayla cried. "Give me a break."

Archer almost took back her apology. Then she heard Jade's voice in her head:

Listen to her. Try to understand where she's coming from.

Okay, fine. Maybe Archer *was* talking too much about herself.

"You're right." She nodded. "I'm sorry."

Her sister looked as stunned as if Archer had said she wanted to join the cheerleading squad.

"I'm really sorry, Makayla." Archer bit her nails. "I never should have done it. But I was mad. We used to be such good friends...What happened?"

To Archer's absolute mortification, her voice cracked with emotion.

"Don't cry if that stupid eyeliner isn't waterproof," Makayla said.

Archer wiped at her eyes. Sure enough, the eyeliner streaked across her hands.

"See, that's why I need you," she half laughed. "To teach me things like that. I know you have your own life and your own friends, but…" Her face felt hot. "I miss you."

Makayla blinked. "Are you being serious right now?"

"Yeah," she admitted. "I want to be your sister again."

Makayla sat in interminable silence, then finally said, "Start by being a little nicer."

Archer's mouth dropped open. "Me?!"

"Yes, you," her sister scoffed. "You've had this stinky attitude for, like, years now. You're mad at the world. We get it. But nobody wants to be friends with that."

Archer swallowed hard.

It was true. Together, she and Wanda were angry and toxic. She'd already decided that once she got back home, she'd try to make new friends.

"You glare at people like you want to punch them," Makayla continued. "You don't give anyone a chance."

Archer ducked her head. True too. She had judged Jade before she'd even opened her mouth—out of fear Jade would judge her.

"Is that all?" Archer whispered.

"No. You're *such* a faker with Mom and Dad. You show up with all these perfect grades? Give me a break. No one *gets* math, okay?"

"I do," Archer said eagerly. "I could help you."

Makayla gave her a suspicious look. "Why?"

"Because," Archer said, surprised. "You're my sister."

Makayla sat in silence for a long moment. "I haven't been much of a sister to you, lately, have I?" She sighed, the soda sweet on her breath. "Look, Archer, I'm sorry. Things aren't always easy for me either."

Archer nodded, thinking back to some of the more personal messages Makayla had written to Paolo.

"Sometimes I get so mad at you." Makayla looked down at her manicured nails. "I work so hard to fit in, and you don't bother with it at all. Sometimes I wish I could be like that." She shrugged. "But that's not your fault and I'm sorry."

Archer was so stunned, she couldn't speak.

She wishes she could be like me?

"I'm sorry too." She picked at a loose string on her trousers. "Do you think we could be friends?"

"Uggh." Makayla took a long drink. "This is so awkward."

Archer gave a nervous laugh. "Excruciating."

Her sister hopped to her feet and tried the doorknob. "It's unlocked."

For the millionth time in the past few days, Archer remembered the moment she'd nearly locked her sister out in the freezing cold.

I'm done being that person.

Makayla fidgeted with her necklace. Then she looked at Archer. "Yeah, we can be friends. We're *so* not going to be BFFs. But there's a small chance I might let you hang out with me once in a while." She dropped the silly version of the peace sign that used to be their secret handshake. "In fact, I think we can be sisters again," she said, and flounced out of the room.

Archer slid down to the floor as the other Fireflies rushed in.

"How did it go?" they whispered, clustering around her.

"It went…" Archer's mind reeled, thinking of all the things her sister had said. "It went okay."

Jade looked disappointed. "Just okay?"

"Look, she didn't turn me into a frog." Archer shrugged. "So, I think it's a win."

The Fireflies laughed.

Things with her sister might not be perfect. They might not even be great. But they were definitely going to get better.

For that—for now—she was grateful.

Chapter Forty

Isla's cheeks hurt from pretending to smile. It was the night of the big dance, and her parents still refused to give her permission.

"Darling, you know better," her mother had tsked. "Why would that be acceptable at camp when it's not acceptable at home?"

It was what she'd expected, but it didn't make it hurt less that she wouldn't see Jordan again. She imagined him on the dance floor, decked out in a shirt and tie. He would look for her and—her heart sank—be disappointed.

Isla kept the news to herself until the other Fireflies had finished dinner. She was so upset that she couldn't even look up at the competition board, though they must have had a good lead since Lauren was smiling when they left the mess hall.

"I'm so excited to go to the dance." Lauren had a skip in her step. "Isla, I can't wait to wear that black dress."

Isla had brought two dresses to camp and had promised to let Lauren borrow the one with the flirty skirt and bows on the sleeves.

"You'll look great," Isla said bravely.

The buses were already parked in the lot outside the mess hall. They would leave at seven on the dot. Since Isla was not allowed to go, she'd have to play board games at the Lodge with one of the counselors.

"Actually..." She stopped walking. "Lauren, wear which-ever dress you want. My parents won't let me go."

Lauren stopped short. "Oh no. I'm so sorry."

"In some ways, it's a relief," Isla admitted. "I'm not allowed to date until I'm older, and to be honest, I didn't like how sneaking out, kissing a boy, and doing things I wasn't supposed to made me feel." She looked at Archer. "Dorky, but true."

Archer lifted her palms. "Hey. I know *exactly* what you mean."

The Fireflies stood in silence.

"Have fun." Isla shrugged. "Just don't tell me if he dances with other girls."

She took off down the path. Lauren, Jade, and Archer whispered behind her, but she didn't stop. Too much sympathy would make her cry.

It all felt deeply unfair. The last thing she wanted was to stay in the cabin and watch the other Fireflies get dressed up, piling on hairspray, lip gloss, and Jade's perfume.

She climbed the cabin steps two by two and slid under the scratchy wool blanket on her bed before the other girls had even passed the front door.

Focus on the positives: I own a business, I'm head of the honor roll, a boy I liked liked me back, I'm respecting my parents...and I have great friends.

Speaking of, they were being suspiciously quiet.

The blanket was either an efficient noise blocker or the other Fireflies were working overtime to not have too much fun getting ready. She peered over the edge of her bed and jumped. The three of them stood there, grinning.

"What are you doing?" she asked, sitting up.

Lauren stretched. "It's a terrible night for a dance."

"*Any* night is a terrible night for a dance," Archer added.

"So..." Jade shrugged. "We decided we could spend the evening getting all dressed up for no reason at all..."

"Or stay here." Archer popped a piece of chocolate into her mouth. "With you."

Isla could not believe it. Lauren, Jade, and Archer would give up the dance—the colorful lights, the glitter, the *fun*—for *her*?

"No," she insisted. "You can't miss the dance! I forbid it."

"She forbids it," Archer chortled. "Isla, you kill me."

Lauren waved her hand, the Firefly bracelet flashing on her wrist. "We can, and we will."

"Besides, there's always next year," Jade said. "I bet you can convince your parents to look at the educational implications of coed harmony by then."

"To next year!" Archer thrust her fist into the air.

Lauren looked at the floor as the other girls cheered. She

was probably thinking about how long the year would be. Isla thought about it all the time.

Hopping out of bed, she hugged each of the Fireflies tight. Suddenly, she was grateful her parents were stubborn. Instead of fawning over boys, she could focus on what really mattered: her friends.

"You guys are the best," she said. "Let's go play board games. Archer, I might even let you beat me."

Jade cleared her throat. "First, there's something I'd like to do."

Chapter Forty-One

The other Fireflies looked at Jade.

"What's up?" Archer asked.

"Remember when we had that ceremony for Kiara?" Jade frowned. "I...I'd like to do it again."

Lauren touched her hand. "You sure? You seemed pretty upset last time."

"I was. This time, though, I'm ready to say goodbye."

Ever since she'd gotten the letter from Cat, she felt different. The image of Kiara calling her a traitor was replaced with the truth—Kiara had wanted to stay friends.

The girls studied her in solemn silence. Then Archer nodded. "What do you need us to do?"

* * *

The Fireflies got permission from Cassandra to spend thirty minutes at the shore before reporting to the Lodge. The beach was empty. The Fireflies stood at the edge of the water in silence.

Letting out a deep breath, Jade faced her friends.

"Archer?" she said.

Archer stepped forward. In a low voice, she repeated the speech Lauren had made that first time. One by one, each of the Fireflies then went around and told their favorite stories Jade had shared about Kiara.

"I like the one where you and Kiara save the puppy," Lauren said.

Jade smiled, remembering.

"Stuffing," Jade said. "We named him Stuffing because we found him right after Thanksgiving. I think I'll go see him when I get home."

The other stories also made Jade laugh, like the one where she and Kiara had gone to school dressed up as boys, the time they had a brussels-sprout-eating contest, and when she'd wrapped Kiara's birthday present with so much duct tape that it had taken a whole hour to get into it. The memories filled her heart with joy, especially to think that the Fireflies could talk about Kiara like they'd known her. Finally, Jade pulled out a sheet of paper. Her heart ached as she studied it.

"I'm going to read a poem. This one means a lot to me."

The previous fall, Kiara had won a poetry competition. It was announced at assembly, and she was so shocked she couldn't stop giggling. The teachers had wanted her to read the winning poem, but since she had the giggles, she'd had to start over three times. Eventually, she got serious, leaned into the microphone, and her words had echoed across the gymnasium.

"In Time"

Age is all around me.

Candles in my cake, yearbooks, report cards that rate
what I do.
Do I measure up, stand tall, make them proud?
When I worry
The bird sings on the cherry tree,
The water glass, half full, dances on my desk,
And we laugh at everything and
Nothing.
Fears fade away, into the dark of day, and
The sun, oh
the sun
Is so bright with you.
Worries fade and now we
Celebrate
We celebrate these days.

"How beautiful," Lauren whispered.

"It was about our friendship. I was thinking about the words and it hit me—" She looked up at the sky.

We celebrate these days.

"Kiara was the most kind, generous, giving person. For too long, I was afraid her final words summed up our friendship, but they didn't."

The other Fireflies murmured their agreement.

"Our friendship is that poem and everywhere I look. A thousand things I see and think and feel. So..." Jade closed her eyes, imagining Kiara as the water, the sky, and the sparkle in the sun. "I love you and miss you. I know you want the best for me, and I'm going to make you proud of me. Rest in peace, Kiara."

Jade pulled out a pair of scissors from her bag. She handed them to Archer and indicated the friendship bracelets on her arm.

"You sure?" Archer whispered.

Jade nodded.

With a solemn snip, the weight of the bracelets fell from her arm and dropped into the sand. She handed Lauren the bracelet from that first day. Lauren looked surprised but then tied it to Jade's wrist.

"I'm sorry it took so long," Jade murmured.

Lauren squeezed her hand. It looked like she wanted to say something, but instead, she choked up and turned away.

"Group hug," Archer demanded.

The Fireflies rushed in. It took a minute for Lauren to turn and join them.

"Thank you for doing this," Jade told her friends. "You are the reason we celebrate these days."

Then, since the whole point was to *stop* feeling gloomy, she looked at Lauren's watch and gave a dramatic shriek.

"It's been forty-five minutes. We are in so much trouble. Archer, race you to the Lodge?"

Archer took off running, and the girls ran after her, squealing with laughter, but Lauren's laughter rang false.

"You okay?" Jade asked, catching up to her as she struggled with her ankle.

Lauren avoided her gaze. "That was really beautiful."

Jade grabbed her hand. "Thank you for doing it."

Archer turned and waved. "Come on, slowpokes!" she shouted.

"Let's go," Lauren cried.

They took off. Even though Lauren was laughing, something was definitely bothering her.

But what?

Chapter Forty-Two

Lauren sat on the couch at movie night, fighting tears. She'd had a hard time keeping it together ever since Jade had put on that friendship bracelet the night before, at Kiara's ceremony. It almost broke her heart. Not to mention how brave Archer had been this week, confronting her sister, and Isla, accepting her parents' rules.

The smell of freshly buttered popcorn wafted through the room. Lauren looked up. Chef had arrived and was laying out paper bags of popcorn on one of the side tables, next to bottles of soda.

"Snacks are here," Cassandra called. "Everyone grab your popcorn and something to drink if you want it, and we'll get started."

Lauren followed the other Fireflies to the snack table. The girls loaded up on popcorn while she stared blankly at a green container of Sprite.

"Hello, missy." Chef gave a cheerful wave.

That's all it took—the tears started.

"Can I talk to you?" she asked in a strangled whisper.

Chef said something to Cassandra, who took over at the table. Then Chef nodded at Lauren.

"Let's step outside."

Isla, Jade, and Archer were headed back to the couch.

"Let me tell the girls." Lauren rushed up and tapped Isla's shoulder. "I'm going to go talk to Chef."

"Hurry," Archer called. "I'm going to open the candy."

The candy.

Archer's mother had sent yet another shipment, this time a huge bag of miniature candy bars. Lauren could picture the girls devouring every piece, while shoving handfuls of buttery popcorn into their mouths.

These girls have no idea how lucky they are.

"See you in a minute," Lauren said, and headed for the door.

Outside, it was getting dark. Chef sat at the picnic table overlooking the lake. The mosquitoes attacked Lauren the second she sat down. She slapped them away in frustration.

"They don't bite me." Chef chuckled. "I'm too mean."

"Not true." Lauren hopped up to grab a can of bug spray from the supply bucket by the front door. The familiar pine scent coated her skin. She would never be able to use bug spray again without thinking about camp.

"So, what's on your mind, missy?" Chef asked.

Lauren stared down at her hands. She still hadn't told Chef that the administration had turned down her request to volunteer in the kitchen. Voice flat, she shared the bad news.

"Unbelievable," she cried. "They don't know their heads from their bottom halves!"

Lauren gave a weak smile. "I won't get to see the girls again. This is it, for me."

"Oh, missy." Chef sighed. "You're so much like me."

"What do you mean?" Lauren said.

Chef squinted out at the water. "My family came over from Ireland when I was ten. My parents got sick almost right away and died within two months of each other. They were too proud to go to the hospital because they couldn't pay, you see. So, me and my two brothers had nowhere to go. The state put us into separate orphanages. I never saw them again."

Lauren put her hand to her mouth.

"So, one day," Chef continued, "this woman showed up. She was in her sixties, but she wanted to adopt a girl. They lined us up like cattle at an auction house. We were supposed to stand up straight, look smart, and say 'yes ma'am,' but when she spoke to me, I stuck my tongue out at her." Chef grinned. "That woman became my mother."

Lauren pressed her hands together. "Wow."

For years, she'd dreamed about something like that happening to her. Eventually, she'd accepted the fact that she was on her own.

"That woman changed my life," Chef said. "I was in for five years, missy, the longest five years of my life. I'm telling you this to say…" She held Lauren's gaze. "I know what you're going through, and I'm sorry."

Lauren nodded, throat tight.

"Those girls." Chef gestured at the building. "They don't know what they have."

"I know," she whispered. "Sometimes, I get so mad at them. It isn't right. They're my best friends."

Chef shook her head. "It's okay to feel that way."

Lauren picked at the surface of the picnic table. "Should I tell them? The truth?"

"That's something you'll have to decide for yourself, missy." Chef patted her arm. "In my experience, love is love, warts and all."

Lauren gave Chef a clumsy hug and headed back inside. At the threshold, she hesitated.

What should I do? Should I tell them?

The girls would never understand. Not really.

Straightening her shoulders, Lauren headed to the couch and took her seat.

"Candy?" Archer asked.

Lauren nodded. "Thanks." She reached for a Crunch bar.

Isla caught her up on what she'd missed. Lauren sat back and watched the movie, laughing with everyone else. At one point, Jade reached over and squeezed her hand.

Lauren felt frozen against the scratchy cushions, despite the hot tears threatening to spill down her cheeks. Even though she was surrounded by her best friends, she'd never felt lonelier in her life.

* * *

That night, Cassandra was out with the other counselors, and the Fireflies were snuggled in their bunks. Lauren stared out the window at the lake, Chef's words ringing in her ears, and reflected on how brave each of the Fireflies had been this summer.

It's my turn.

"Fireflies," she said in a choked whisper. "I have to tell you something."

In a low tone, she confessed to everything—her "family" didn't exist. She lived in a group foster home. She was an orphan.

The words came tumbling out. As they did, Lauren felt a weight lifting from her heart. Like she was finally free.

"I thought I'd be embarrassed to tell." Lauren twisted the sheets around her hand, watching a firefly dance over the water. "I'm relieved, though. You're my best friends. You deserve to know."

There was a sound at the edge of the bed, and she turned. The other Fireflies stood there, and they hugged her tight. Then Archer squeezed her hands.

"I'm so glad you told us, but I already knew."

"Wh-what?" Lauren stammered. "How?"

The funny looks Archer had been giving her jumped into her mind.

"I opened your mail," Archer said. "There was—"

"You did what?" Isla cried. "Archer, that's a federal offense."

"It was an *accident*. Anyway. I knew, but I'm so glad you trusted us enough to tell us yourself."

Relief filled Lauren's heart. "Thank you."

"What was it like growing up there?" Isla asked. "Was it like *Annie?*"

Lauren snorted. "Not at all." Trying to keep it light, she told them stories about her past. The girls seemed outraged that she never got presents for Christmas or her birthday.

Jade shook her head. "Tell me when it's your birthday, because you're definitely getting something from me."

Lauren shrugged. "I have a roof over my head. I don't need anything else."

"Uggh." Isla smoothed the lapel of her designer shirt. "You must think we are such brats."

Lauren flushed. "Sometimes. But really, I think it's our differences that make us such good friends. It's important for you guys to know that I'm not coming back next year, but I still want to stay in touch. You're my best friends. I don't want to lose you."

"You won't." Archer's voice was fierce.

Jade held up her arm, showcasing her bracelet. "We're Fireflies, Lauren."

Isla nodded. "That means we're best friends. Forever."

"Bring it in," Archer said.

Lauren brought her hand in to meet the others. She was happy the girls knew the truth and still loved her for her, but it didn't change the fact that everything was ending.

"Zap, zap, zap," they cried.

Lauren shouted along with them. For the first time ever, though, she didn't picture a firefly lighting up. Instead, she imagined a light fading into darkness.

Chapter Forty-Three

Archer, Jade, and Isla huddled around the red table in the cabin. It was early morning. Cassandra had already left to help out with breakfast, and Lauren was out on her walk. There was still time before she would return with donuts, so Archer had called a secret meeting of the Fireflies.

"So, I wanted to talk about the thing with Lauren." She picked at a chipped piece of paint on the table. "How are you guys feeling?"

"Sad," Isla said. "I can't believe we're never going to see her again."

"I know." Archer glanced at Lauren's empty bunk. "I wanted to try to figure something out."

"You mean, to get her back here next year?" Jade asked. "We could set up a crowdfunding campaign," Isla cried. "Raise money for her!"

It was a good idea, but Jade shook her head. "She'd never accept it."

Too true.

Once, when Archer had brought Lauren ice cream back from the canteen, she had waved off the dollar bill Lauren had tried to hand her, and Lauren had had a fit. She'd made a big deal out being able to pay and insisted Archer take the money.

"Maybe we should just..." Archer fought the lump in her throat. "Let her know how we feel about her. If we have to say goodbye. But how?"

"The essay," Jade whispered. "For the Faces of Blueberry Pine competition. She planned for us to write one about what we've learned from the contest, which we could still do. But we could write another one in secret. One about Lauren."

"The competition!" Archer groaned, burying her face in her hands. "*That's* why she wanted to win so bad. She wants something to remind her of her time here. Of us."

"Then we will *win*." Isla dark eyes flashed. "I'll write the rough draft. My parents have been sending me to college prep courses for years. I can write an essay in my sleep."

"We can't mention she's an orphan," Archer warned. "It's not something she wants everyone to know."

"We'll just say what she means to us," Jade agreed.

"She means everything," Archer said. "Without her, the Fireflies wouldn't exist."

Outside, raindrops started to splash against the front porch.

"This weather is perfect." Isla hopped to her feet and shut

the window. "Canoeing will get canceled this afternoon, so I can get started then."

"Perfect. Bring it in," Archer said, and the Fireflies put their hands in the center. "This time, it's for Lauren."

The Fireflies gave a solemn nod. "For Lauren."

Chapter Forty-Four

Isla settled into a chair in the computer lab and stared down at the keyboard, waiting for inspiration to strike. It didn't take long. The most difficult part about nonfiction writing, she'd learned, was the structure. Inserting the facts was easy.

With Lauren, the facts were simple: her leadership was the reason the summer had been a success. The Fireflies were best friends because of her, and as a result, each one of them had become a better version of themselves. Personally, Isla couldn't believe how much she had changed.

Resting her hand on her chin, she looked out the window at the forest. The mist made the ferns shine, sunshine filtered through the leaves in spite of the light rain, and she could practically hear the sound of the frogs croaking by the lake. The scene filled her with a sense of peace, so different from the panic of those first few weeks.

I was so scared of everything. Now, I don't feel scared of anything.

Breaking up with Jordan was the hardest thing she'd ever done. More difficult than starting a business, singing onstage in front of the boys, and even more difficult than finding the courage to come to camp at all. In spite of how much she liked him, Isla had decided to respect her parents' rules about dating and hadn't looked back.

As much as I'll miss the other Fireflies, I'll be glad to get back home.

Back to the honking cabs, the hiss of the grates on the sidewalk, and the sizzle of fried onions from the vendors on the street corners. To the museums, the symphonies, and her apartment with the doorman.

Once again, Isla looked out at the forest. She would have to pay more attention to the outdoors back home. She could go to Central Park. Make an effort to be outside. Stop hiding all the time behind her business and her studies.

And when I get off course, I'll have the Fireflies to guide me back home.

After Lauren had revealed her secret, the Fireflies made a vow to video chat the first Thursday of every month. Lauren had seemed worried about it, so Isla explained it was possible to video chat at the library, as long as she brought a headset and spoke quietly. Even if Lauren couldn't be there next summer, Isla was determined to keep Lauren in her life.

She will *be there, in spirit. I am going to write an essay that will make sure we are the faces of Blueberry Pine.*

Isla lowered her hands to the keyboard and got started.

* * *

Once the Fireflies had seen the rough draft of the essay, Isla polished it three times. They worked fast and secretly, slipping copies under one another's pillows; in their dressers; and now, under their trays at dinner. Lauren stood at the hot bar, getting a second helping of lasagna, so they were safe.

"Go through and make changes," Isla whispered. "The deadline's tomorrow morning. I'll rewrite it and turn it in."

Lauren headed back their way, and the other Fireflies returned to ranking flavors of ice cream—the conversation that had dominated dinner. The final debate was between rocky road (Archer and Isla) and chocolate chip cookie dough (Jade).

"Lauren." Archer pointed at her. "You haven't said a thing, so you get the final vote. Which one wins?"

Lauren fiddled with her bracelet. "I'm Switzerland. I'm neutral."

"Come on!" Archer slammed her hands against the table, sloshing soda out of everyone's glasses. "I know you've had them both."

Lauren's cheeks colored. "I…" She set down her fork, looking lost, when Isla realized something.

"You've never had them," she said, surprised. "Have you?"

Jade gave her a warning look. "Not everyone has tried every flavor of ice cream on the planet!"

Lauren fiddled with her fork. Her expression was pained.

Wow. Simple things that I take for granted, like silly flavors of ice cream, are completely outside her world of experience.

What would that be like? To miss out on things like cookie dough ice cream and rocky road? To not have a family?

Isla's heart ached. To think she had spent the summer complaining about her parents and their rules while Lauren didn't have a family at all.

"I'm sorry, Lauren." Isla folded her hands. "We do have better things to talk about. You might not believe me, but we do."

Isla exchanged a brief look with Jade and Archer. She would work through the night on the essay. It had to win.

For once, Lauren deserved to have something go her way.

Chapter Forty-Five

Jade checked the mail. To her surprise, a familiar navy envelope sat in the box.

Colin.

He'd stopped writing to her weeks ago.

Heart pounding, she grabbed the envelope and stared at it in silence. Then, clear as day, she heard Kiara say, *The suspense. Open it, already!*

Jade smiled.

Ever since the ceremony on the beach, it had felt like Kiara was there, helping her see the world for the better. So many things seemed funny now, instead of sad.

It felt so strange, in fact, that Jade had set up an impromptu appointment to talk to her therapist about these unexpected feelings.

"I'm proud of you, Jade." Mrs. Anderson nodded. "You're letting go."

"It's weird, though, right?" she worried. "I keep imagining she's there. Imagining the things she would say to me."

The therapist shook her head. "It's fine. When you're away from the other Fireflies, you'll probably think of them too."

Jade pictured being back at school, imagining Archer saying all sorts of hilarious things.

"It feels good thinking about Kiara," Jade said. "I don't want to forget her."

Mrs. Anderson nodded. "That's understandable. She only wanted the best for you."

Letting out a deep breath, Jade opened the letter from Colin.

Dear Jade,

You have excelled at ignoring my letters. Camp must be too fun to bother writing to a boring old chap like me. Now that the fun is almost over, I hope you'll pick up the phone when I call. If not, I totally get it and will leave you alone. But you can't blame a guy for trying.

Colin

Jade cradled the paper in her hands.

He's going to callll you...I think he looooves you...

Jade grinned, imagining Kiara doing some ridiculous victory dance. Then she hopped to her feet and headed toward the Lodge. She couldn't wait to tell her friends about Colin.

Chapter Forty-Six

Lauren stared into the bathroom mirror as she pulled her hair up into a wet ponytail. During swim hour, she'd thought so much about that first day when the other Fireflies had pranked Makayla. It seemed like mere moments had passed, but in some ways, it seemed like forever. So much had happened, and so much had changed.

The friendship she'd formed with Jade, Archer, and Isla was not something she could walk away from like she'd once planned. Instead, it meant opening a space in her heart for the hurt that would come with missing them, along with the knowledge that they would still be there, even from far away. She planned to enjoy every second of the two days they had left together, but couldn't help but take a moment to feel sad about the Faces of Blueberry Pine competition.

The final ceremony was scheduled in the mess hall during Indoor Rec, so the counselors could use the stage. During soccer, one of the Cardinals told Lauren that she'd heard the essay contest finalists had been invited to read their essays during the ceremony. Since the Fireflies hadn't heard anything, that meant they were out of the running for the essay contest. Worse, it was rumored that the Bluebirds would perform. That would put them at the head of the leaderboard, and they would win the whole thing.

Lauren was devastated.

The Faces of Blueberry Pine afforded one group of friends the priceless opportunity to be frozen in time, to commemorate this summer for years to come. It would have meant everything to share that with the other girls. Unfortunately, it wasn't going to work out that way.

"You ready, Lauren?" Jade called. "We have to get to the final ceremony."

Most of the other campers had already left the changing room and headed to the mess hall. The other Fireflies hovered at the door, looking hopeful. Lauren didn't have the heart to tell them it was over.

"Let's go," she said. "See who won this thing."

On the walk to the mess hall, Isla glanced over her shoulder and gave her a big smile, practically running into a tree in the process. The Fireflies giggled and linked arms. Jade started singing a silly version of one of the camp songs, and Archer joined in.

Lauren was quiet during the walk. The silly singing, the crunch of wood chips under their feet, and even the squeak of Archer's boots seemed like a ticking clock, marching her farther away from the best summer of her life.

They're the greatest. I'm going to miss them so much.

The mess hall loomed into sight, and Jade raised her fist to the sky. "Let's do this," she cried.

The tables had all been pushed aside, and chairs had been set up to look like an auditorium. The Fireflies took a seat by the Butterflies, and Lauren tried not to look over at the Bluebirds, who were chanting a funny rhyme. At the beginning of the summer, it had sounded like a different language. Now, she knew every word.

The birds cheep tweedle-deet,

the birds cheep tweedle-dumb

Roll me over the finch's shoulder

Let's have fun!

Taylor climbed onstage, microphone in hand. She started the camp song and quickly, the campers joined in. Too many emotions welled up in Lauren's heart. She blinked furiously, fighting back tears, and a hand gripped hers.

Isla.

"I'm going to miss everything about this," Isla whispered.

Lauren squeezed her hand hard.

"Ladies, it's the moment we've all been waiting for!" Taylor roared. "The finalists in our essay contest! As you know, the judges awarded each essay a point value, and the totals have been combined with your previous scores. Following the essay finalists, we will announce the grand-prize winner, the lucky campers who will be the Faces of Blueberry Pine."

Archer fidgeted. "It better not go to Makayla."

Lauren cringed. "If it does, we still have one another."

"Forget the Bluebirds," Jade insisted. "We still have a chance."

Isla gave a vigorous nod, patting Lauren on the knee.

Lauren shook her head. How had they not heard the rumor? She should tell them, so they didn't get their hopes up. She had just opened her mouth to speak when Cassandra joined Taylor onstage and called up the first finalist.

"Kiwi Cabin," she cried.

The crowd cheered, and Lauren looked at the younger team. The Kiwis had never placed before. Maybe it was possible to...

Don't think like that. It's over.

One of the Kiwis walked to the stage. She seemed prepared. So the rumor was true.

Lauren sat back in her chair with a thump. The essay from Kiwi Cabin was cute. It was all about the experiences the girls had shared around the campfire, canoeing on the lake, and telling ghost stories late at night. It was like a love poem to Blueberry Pine and easy to see how it had placed.

The Finches took third place. Their essay was a hilarious take on the counselors. Lauren found herself giggling in spite of her mood.

Chuckling, Taylor got back on the mic. "Two more...first up, the Bluebirds!"

"Uggh." Archer stomped her boots. "I'm telling you, this thing is *rigged.*"

Makayla gave a catlike smile, then read a sentimental piece about the power of nature. It was pretty basic, but the campers listened, rapt.

Lauren's heart was heavy. "The Bluebirds won."

Jade shook her head. "It's not over."

Taylor squinted out at the audience. "Our final essay is a heartfelt piece that truly captures the power of friendship at Blueberry Pine." She handed the mic to Cassandra, who looked at Lauren and smiled.

"Fireflies, are you ready?"

Lauren sat up straight. "Wait. What?"

Jade giggled. "Hang on to your chair. This one's for you."

Lauren watched in confusion. What was happening?

Jade ran down the aisle. She climbed onstage, took the mic, and touched her bracelet. Then she started to read.

"'There are moments in life where magic happens. The flash of a firefly in the woods, the spark of laughter between new friends, the moment you realize you've met someone destined to change your life. The moment Lauren walked into Firefly Cabin, in a tornado of red hair and laughter, I knew—just like every girl in our cabin knew—our lives would be changed forever.'"

Lauren put her hands to her mouth. "What is this?" she breathed.

"Listen," Isla whispered, and Archer grabbed her hand.

Lauren sat in shock as Jade told the story of four different girls, each facing private struggles but strengthened by her leadership.

"'Lauren is the head Firefly,'" Jade read. "'Our brightest light. Even though we will be separated in just a few days, the light of our friendship will burn forever. The odds are good we won't all be back at camp next year, for different reasons...'" Jade seemed to fight back tears. "'But thanks to Lauren, the distance that separates us won't matter, because this summer in Firefly Cabin has formed a sisterhood that cannot be broken.' Thank you."

Jade folded the paper and handed the mic back to Cassandra.

The silence was deafening. Then the campers burst into thunderous applause. They hooted and hollered, feet stamping against the ground until the building practically shook.

Cassandra shouted, "Well, I guess it's clear! The first-place winner of the essay contest is Firefly Cabin. Which gives the Fireflies enough points to surpass our second-place essay winner, the Bluebirds. Fireflies, come on up here!"

"Hold on." Lauren felt like she was dreaming. "What does she mean?"

"We won," Archer shrieked. "We beat my *sister*. We won we won we won. *Go!*"

Lauren ran onto the stage. She didn't realize tears were streaming down her face until Jade brushed them away. Then Archer grabbed Lauren's hand and held it up into the air.

The crowd went wild.

"I can't believe you guys did this," Lauren cried as the other Fireflies clustered around her.

Archer whacked her on the back. "You happy?"

Lauren beamed. "You have no idea."

Through the window, the sun danced off the lake as Taylor gave them high fives. Then camp president Barbara Middleton shook their hands and offered her congratulations, though she gave a slight frown after meeting Archer. She whispered something to Taylor.

There was no time to wonder why, though, because Cassandra gleefully congratulated them. "How does it feel, ladies? You're going to be the Faces of Blueberry Pine!"

Lauren shook her head. "Amazing." She burst into tears, remembering the time she'd spent studying the website and brochure, wondering what camp would be all about.

"Lauren..." Isla squeezed her hand. "Are you okay?"

The girls circled around her. She looked into the faces of her friends, her sisters. The words of the essay were right—no matter what happened, the bond between the Fireflies would last forever.

Chapter Forty-Seven

Beating the Bluebirds was like something out of a comic book where good versus evil go head-to-head, and good prevails. Archer made eye contact with her sister the moment the Fireflies were declared the winner. Makayla was so mad! Her face flushed hot pink, and there was so much huffing and hair tossing it was a wonder her head didn't roll off. Archer blew a kiss in her direction, which her sister pretended to not see.

Once the ceremony had ended, the campers had some time before electives, so the Fireflies went back to the cabin to store the essay in a safe place. Jade, Archer, and Isla wanted Lauren to take it home at the end of camp.

Lauren's plan was more interactive. "We'll pass it back and forth through the mail. Because I don't just want to get emails from you guys, I want letters."

"Or you could just chat with our picture on the website," Jade suggested. "Or the brochure. Heck, we're going to be everywhere. Ooh, we should suggest billboards."

The Fireflies chanted, sang, and cheered all the way back to the cabin. There, they jumped up and down once again. They stopped when Cassandra banged in through the door, her face like thunder.

"Archer, I need to see you outside."

Archer looked at the other Fireflies in surprise. Was she in trouble or something? Her parents *had* gotten into town early—they were probably suffering from Makayla withdrawals—and planned to take her and her sister out to dinner. Archer had agreed to go on the condition that she made it back in time for the late-night bonfire and could bring the girls a pizza, but maybe she should have checked with Cassandra first.

"Okay." Archer swallowed hard. "What's up?"

Cassandra didn't speak until they were a few feet away from the cabin, under one of the tall pine trees. "I have bad news."

Archer's mouth dropped open. "You tallied wrong? The Bluebirds won?"

Cassandra looked confused. "No. It's…" Then to Archer's complete shock, her counselor let out a cuss word. "The administration wants you to dye your hair. Barbara Middleton was *quote* dismayed *unquote* to discover one of the winners had blue and purple hair. I'm so sorry, Archer. You're an individual, I respect you, and I can't believe I have to tell you this."

Archer was shocked. Not by the message—she'd suspected the administration would take issue with her hair from day one. The thing that shocked her was that Cassandra was so…cool about it. Embarrassed, she looked down at her combat boots.

"No worries," she mumbled. "I'll figure it out."

Turning, she walked back into the cabin.

"That was quick." Lauren looked confused. "What happened?"

Archer breathed in the familiar scent of the room. It was so rustic and something she'd grown to love. "So, the administration wants me to change my hair. Cover up the streaks or I'm out."

The other Fireflies, who were in the middle of raiding a bag of M&M's, stopped short.

"Dye your hair?" Lauren whispered.

Jade dropped an M&M back into the bag. "You're kidding."

"I'm not surprised." Isla smoothed her bangs. "They're so strict about the uniform. They wouldn't want to advertise wacky hair."

Archer glared at her. "Uh, whose side are you on?"

"Yours, of course." Isla looked puzzled. "I'm just saying..."

"They want something timeless." Jade wadded up a candy wrapper. "You know it, we all know it. That one picture was on the brochure forever."

Archer bit her nail. It wasn't that she minded changing her hair—she'd planned on doing that when she got back home—it was just...

"I can't let them oppress my individuality. Look, I'll cheer you on at the photo shoot, but you'll have to do it without me." The girls protested, but she held up her hand. "Sorry. That's the way it is."

There wasn't time to discuss it further since the Fireflies had to get to their electives. During her final ropes course class, Archer felt resolute in her decision. It was a bummer, though, because everyone kept congratulating her.

Even Makayla was gracious about her win, when she came to pick Archer up at the cabin later that evening. Through the screen, Makayla gave a perfunctory wave.

"Congratulations on being the Faces of Blueberry Pine," she said. "Looks like you won fair and square. Archer, you ready?"

"I'll see you guys soon," Archer said, and headed outside.

Makayla gave her a sidelong look. "No gloating?"

"There's nothing to gloat about." Archer stomped down the steps. "Trust me."

* * *

In the parking lot, Archer hugged her parents tight. It was hard to believe it had been only eight weeks. It felt like years since she'd seen them.

The restaurant was crowded, and they squeezed through tiny tables to a booth by a window. Once their order of cheesy breadsticks had arrived at the table, Makayla moved on from chattering about the Bluebirds to the competition.

"It was this huge thing. Then she had to go and win it all." Makayla hooked her thumb in Archer's direction. Weirdly, she looked proud.

"Honey, that's great." Her mother ruffled her hair. "Are you excited?"

"Not anymore," she said, and explained the ultimatum.

Makayla let out a low whistle. "What are you going to do?"

"Don't know." Archer bit into some melted cheese. "It's an attack on my personal taste, so…"

"How could it be?" Makayla waved a straw. "You don't have any."

"I have enough to know you look like Hello Kitty with that eye shadow."

Makayla laughed, batting her pink and silver eyelids. "Good one."

Archer hid a smile as the waiter refilled their waters. For once, the bickering felt fun, not mean. Like jokes between sisters should.

"You need to think long and hard about this," her mom said, passing her another breadstick. "I'd hate to see you miss out on something so special."

Archer wiped a streak of tomato sauce off her hands. She wanted to be in that photo with the other Fireflies more than *anything*. But she didn't know how to back down without looking like a fool.

"I'll live," she grumbled.

Makayla snorted. "Here lies Archer. She could have been the face of Blueberry Pine, but she was too mad at the world. Which was so weird, because the world wasn't mad at her."

Archer took a sip of Coke to hide her annoyance, but she knew Makayla's words were true.

Chapter Forty-Eight

Lauren's heart was heavy as she knocked on the screen door of the kitchen. She couldn't believe she would never see Chef again.

"Hello, missy." Chef opened the door, wiping her hands on her apron. "I didn't expect you'd have time for me today."

"I wanted to give you this."

Lauren held out a carefully wrapped package, and Chef studied it in confusion. "What's this?"

"A present." Lauren lifted her chin, willing herself not to cry. "Because I'm going to miss you."

Chef made a tsking sound. "Of all the wasteful things," she grumbled, but set it on the counter with extra care before pulling out her glasses.

Lauren held her breath as Chef opened the gift. It was a framed collage she'd created during Indoor Rec. It had sparkling, brightly colored pictures of donuts, birthday cakes, onions, music notes, and pretty much anything that symbolized her time in the kitchen with Chef. In the center, Archer had helped her write a note in calligraphy: "Honorary Firefly."

Chef sniffed. "Missy, if you wanted treats for your friends, you could have just asked."

Lauren smiled. Chef's harsh tone couldn't hide her emotion.

Chef sat in silence for a long moment, staring at the collage.

"Well, that settles it." She turned to Lauren. "I have tried to talk myself out of this a hundred times, because goodness knows, you wouldn't want to keep spending time with an old grouch like me, but the idea keeps coming back."

Lauren wrinkled her brow in confusion. "What idea?"

Chef's cheeks flushed, and she got to her feet. "Lauren, how would you like to be my daughter?"

Lauren's legs felt like they might go out from underneath her.

Did I get heatstroke, like Isla warned? Am I imagining this?

"I would like to adopt you," Chef said, when she didn't speak. "If you'd like that too."

"Adopt me?" she whispered.

There were so many times in her life she'd hoped to hear those words. Prayed to hear them, but it had never happened.

Tears pricked the back of her eyes.

"Hey." Chef sounded surprised. "Come on, now." She took Lauren by the shoulder. "Sit." She patted a stool by the counter and poured Lauren a drink of water. "Goodness, if the thought makes you cry, maybe I never should have—"

"No, it's..." Lauren downed the water in one gulp. Then she grabbed Chef's hands. "Do you mean it? Please don't say it if you don't mean it."

"Oh, missy." Chef patted her shoulder. "I mean it. You and me, we're the same."

"I think so, too," Lauren whispered. "You understand me. It's like…there was a reason I came here. Beyond the Fireflies."

Chef gave a firm nod. "I believe we were meant to find each other. Does that mean you'll consider it?"

"There's nothing to consider." Chef's face fell, and Lauren laughed. "No, I mean…because the answer's yes. One hundred percent, yes. I can't think of anything I would want more."

Chef's eyes filled with tears. "Well, aren't we a pair."

Lauren leaped to her feet and hugged her tight.

This time, Chef hugged her back, just like a real mother would.

* * *

The Fireflies stood at the edge of the lake.

It was a perfect evening. The sun glinted off the water, and the sand felt like brown sugar underfoot. The photographer set up her equipment on a heavy wool blanket while a makeup artist laid out a series of brushes and powders on a folding table.

"Come on over, girls," she called.

Lauren looked at her watch. It was seven o'clock, and Archer wasn't there.

She wouldn't ditch the whole thing, would she?

"She'll be here," Jade said as though reading her mind. "I know she will."

The makeup artist applied dark brown mascara to everyone's

lashes and dabbed powder against their faces. It smelled like faded roses, and Lauren giggled.

"I feel like a model."

She also felt like the luckiest girl in the world. Chef had already contacted Shady Acres to request the necessary documents to start the adoption process, as well as permission to escort Lauren back to Arizona on the plane the next morning.

"I won't be needed here," Chef said. "There will be no one to feed once all you rascals are gone. Besides, no daughter of mine is going to fly alone; not if I have anything to say about it."

Daughter of mine.

The words filled her heart with a happiness she'd never dreamed possible.

"We're just about done here..." the makeup artist said, scrutinizing her work.

"We have another girl coming," Jade said quickly. "She is just running late."

Lauren breathed a sigh of relief, until the makeup artist added, "Now, how are you planning to wear your hair?"

The Fireflies exchanged glances. They all had their hair tucked under Blueberry Pine baseball caps.

"Down," Lauren said. "It's humid, though, so I'd like to keep it up until the last possible moment."

The other Fireflies gave a solemn nod.

The makeup artist clicked her tongue. "That won't be long. Once the photographer says she's getting close, we'll have to get started."

Isla froze. "Fireflies, I believe we have company."

Lauren straightened her shoulders as Barbara Middleton approached the counselors on site, along with Carol Kennedy and a group of administrators. Carol Kennedy spotted Lauren and gave a friendly wave.

Just then, Archer ran across the sand.

"You made it," Lauren cried.

"Of course!" Archer hugged them all, her hair hidden beneath her own ball cap. "We're in this together."

"Exactly." Lauren gave an enthusiastic nod. "Which is why...Fireflies?"

Lauren, Jade, and Isla whipped off their caps to reveal streaks of bright blue and purple in their hair. The administrators gasped in surprise. Archer's hand flew to her mouth. "No! You can't be serious."

"So serious." Lauren turned to the administration. "We wanted to thank you for the opportunity to be the Faces of Blueberry Pine. In our experience, Blueberry Pine is a camp designed to empower young women. So, we were surprised when you decided to suppress the individuality of our friend. Archer has her own unique style. That's who she is. You have to accept that, or take the picture without us. What's it going to be?"

The adults looked stunned. Barbara Middleton put her hand to her chest, and Carol Kennedy looked downright ashen. Then Archer stepped forward.

"Wait," she cried. "You guys, look!" She whipped off her cap. Her hair was no longer jet-black, but a warm chestnut

brown, without a streak in sight. "My mom took me to the salon," she murmured. "I couldn't miss out on this."

"You look amazing," Jade said. "Sorry, but you're, like, thirty-five times better-looking than your sister."

"Stop." Archer flushed in delight. "You guys, on the other hand, look terrible. What on Earth were you thinking?"

The Fireflies exploded with laughter. One by one, they pulled off the black wigs Chef had swiped from the theater department, along with the clips of purple and blue hair from the mall the next town over. The administrators let out an audible sigh of relief, and then, Archer turned to face them.

"I did this out of respect for my friends," she said. "But in the future, I hope you guys stop being so narrow-minded. I'm a lot more than a girl with blue and purple hair. To be honest, you're lucky to have me."

The counselors burst into applause, and a few of the adults smiled. Finally, Barbara Middleton stepped forward and shook their hands.

"Girls your age never fail to impress me," she said. "Thank you for the reminder of what matters. You will be an excellent representation of Blueberry Pine."

"It's go time!" The photographer called from down by the beach. She gestured at the sky, where the sun had started to set. It cast a perfect, golden hue.

The makeup artist grabbed her hair wand. "Give me ten minutes." She got to work, and Archer beamed at the Fireflies. Her smile was brighter than the setting sun.

"You guys are ridiculous," she said.

Lauren smiled. "We couldn't do this without you."

As the photographer put them into position, Lauren thought back to the picture on the front cover of the Blueberry Pine brochure. The girls with their arms across one another's shoulders, the laughter and friendship gleaming from their eyes.

It's our turn.

Lauren stood in the center. Jade and Isla stood on either side, arms draped around Lauren, while Archer got down on one knee and lifted her arms to the sky.

"Perfect!" The photographer reached for her camera. "I don't even have to tell you to pretend to be friends."

The girls burst into giggles.

"True." Jade nodded. "We're best friends."

"We've been there for each other every step of the way," Isla said.

Archer grinned at them. "Sometimes, we're nothing but trouble."

Lauren squeezed them close. "In the end, though, we're family."

The camera clicked away, capturing a piece of their history. But it wasn't just history. Lauren thought of her future life with Chef and grinned from ear to ear.

The Fireflies were far from over—their story had just begun.